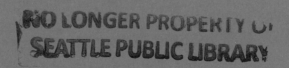

THE SPIDER RING

ANDREW HARWELL

THE SPIDER RING

SCHOLASTIC PRESS | NEW YORK

Library of Congress Control Number: 2014942282

ISBN 978-0-545-68290-9

10 9 8 7 6 5 4 3 2 1   15 16 17 18 19

Printed in the U.S.A.   23
First edition, February 2015

The text type was set in Adobe Caslon Pro.
Book design by Yaffa Jaskoll

TO MY SISTERS

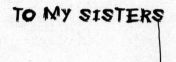

PART ONE

THE BROWN RECLUSE

We are the spiders of the Order of Anansi.

We click and slither and weave our way.

We set our traps through the centuries

And spin our stories from the fabric of time.

CHAPTER 1

Maria had never much cared for spiders.

That was the difference between her and Grandma Esme. Esme *loved* spiders — strangely so. She had pictures of them on everything, from plates and cups to dresses and socks. She had a spider-shaped ring that she never took off — "a gift from an old friend" was all she would say about it. And she wouldn't let Maria or her little brother, Rafi, kill a real spider in her presence. "You never harm a spider," she'd said more than once, "because trust me, children, a spider never forgets."

Grandma Esme's love of spiders wasn't the only strange thing about her. She wore black, silky shawls patterned with stars and planets. She could stand on her head during her morning yoga, even though she had to be at least seventy years old. She owned a collection of fancy whistles, left over from the days when she wasn't Grandma Esme but Esmerelda the Magnificent, the world's tamest lion tamer, at least according to her stories.

She also wore glasses, just like Maria. And just like Maria, she preferred reading to the outdoors.

So while Maria disliked anything with more than four legs — *especially* spiders — she absolutely loved her grandma Esme. Her mom and her brother thought Esme was weird. Maria thought she was, well, *magnificent*.

It was not unusual for Maria to ask, as she did one Friday morning in February, "Mom, can I go to Grandma Esme's house after school?"

Her mother was buried from the waist up in the fridge, scrounging for things to pack for lunch. Now she peeked out at Maria and frowned.

"Again?" she said. "I don't know, *mija*. I feel like I haven't seen you all week."

"I promise I'll be home before dinner. I'll even be here before you get home from work."

Maria's mother was a ranger at Falling Waters, a

park that came all the way up to their backyard. On Fridays, it was so busy with the arrival of weekend campers that Maria's mother had to get to work early and stay even later. While she drove Maria and Rafi to school the rest of the week, on Fridays, they had to ride the bus.

"Can you take your brother with you?" Maria's mother asked her now.

"Take me where?" Rafi asked through a yawn as he stepped into the kitchen. He was wearing the same camo fishing vest he wore every day, and his mess of curly brown hair was particularly unruly.

"To your grandmother's house. I won't be home until after five, so I need you two to stick together."

"I'm almost eleven," Rafi said. "I can take care of myself."

Maria snorted. Just last week, she'd caught him trying to cook a hot dog over the open flame of their stove.

"Plus, I was going to ask if I could go home with Rob after school. His dad said he'd take us fishing in his lake."

Rob McCormick was Rafi's best friend. Unlike the Lopez family, the McCormicks were rich. Instead of living in a small house in a neighborhood where all the small houses looked the same, the McCormicks had fifteen acres of land, including their own lake. Instead of shopping at the secondhand store, they got all their clothes brand-new at the mall.

Another big difference was that Rob's father was alive. He took the boys fishing. It was easy to see why Rafi liked spending time with them.

Maria's mother sighed. "All right," she said. "Maria, you can go to Grandma Esme's, and, Rafi, you can go over to Rob's. But I expect you both to be home in time for dinner. Agreed?"

"Agreed," they said.

"And, Maria, honey, go change your shirt. You've got a hole in your sleeve."

Maria looked down and realized her mom was right. Her favorite shirt, a button-up top with a pattern her grandmother had called "paisley," now had a nickel-sized hole where the left sleeve met the shoulder. She must have ripped it putting it on this morning. She'd have to sew a patch over the hole like she'd done with her jeans and her book bag. She even had a spare purple star that might be a good match. But she hardly had time for that now. The bus was going to be here any minute.

She ran back to her room and threw on the first T-shirt she touched. When she returned, her brother was standing at the front door with their lunches, motioning for her to hurry.

"C'mon, or we'll have to walk," he said.

"Bye, Mom!" Maria called as she ran out the door.

She was in such a rush, she hadn't noticed the spiders that had built webs overnight in the hallway outside her room. Nor had she noticed the cluster of spiders that now hung from the awning above her front door, watching her as she sprinted to catch the bus. And she certainly hadn't noticed the man in the black silk suit who'd been pretending to check the mailbox across the street.

Maria hadn't noticed any of these things. But all of them, waiting, had noticed Maria.

It was going to be a very long day at school.

Maria had a quiz in math, an oral report in social studies, and a solar-system drill in science, all in the same day. But before any of those, she had to survive honors English.

Honors English was Maria's least favorite class. Not

because she didn't like reading or writing, either. Once, in a diary her dad had given her for her birthday, she'd written that she wanted to grow up to be a travel reporter, and have adventures like Agatha, her favorite character from a book. No, the reason Maria hated honors English was that Claire McCormick was in it, too.

Claire was Rob's older sister, but she was as mean as her little brother was nice. While Rafi and Rob were practically inseparable, Maria and Claire couldn't be further from friends. Claire always made fun of Maria's thrift-shop clothes, her vintage glasses, and the fact that she was smart. Maria always said that Claire had followers instead of friends.

Maria stayed out of Claire's way whenever she could, but she couldn't avoid her in honors English. Thanks to the cruel twist of fate known as alphabetical order, Claire sat directly behind Maria, whispering nasty comments whenever Ms. Wainscott wasn't paying attention. Today, Claire was using the time before the bell to brag about her thirteenth birthday party, to which Maria was *not* invited. Looking around, Maria got the feeling she was the only person in her class who wasn't.

"We're going to put a platform over the pool to make a dance floor," Claire said. "I'm already working on the perfect playlist."

"That sounds awesome," said Mark Spitzer, the only boy on both the soccer team and the math club.

"You always make the best playlists," added Tina Brown, whose parents owned a restaurant Maria's family couldn't afford even on special occasions.

It seemed like everyone in seventh grade was in a contest to see who could kiss up to Claire the most. Everyone except Maria and her best friend, Derek — who, unfortunately for Maria, did not take honors English.

No one was mean to Derek, though. Everyone liked Derek because he made people laugh, even teachers. When it came to Maria, who couldn't even make her own mom or brother laugh, people found it easier to side with Claire. It's not like Maria really cared all that much. Grandma Esme said that all the most interesting people were misunderstood during their lifetimes.

"Oh my gosh, Maria, is that *food* on your shirt?"

Maria tried to look over her shoulder at the back of her T-shirt, the one she'd grabbed quickly while getting ready that morning. In the edge of her vision, there appeared to be a mustard stain — probably from when she'd helped Rafi make the hot dogs. Her face flushed with embarrassment as Tina and Mark and the rest of the kids around her snickered. Whatever Grandma Esme said, a lifetime was a long time to be misunderstood.

"You should just put another patch over it," Claire said. "Or maybe a piece of duct tape? I'm sure the janitor has a spare roll you could borrow."

"Wait, Claire, I think you have something on your face," Maria said hotly. "Oh, no, sorry, that *is* your face."

Claire scowled and opened her mouth like she was about to snap back, but thankfully the bell rang, and Ms. Wainscott stepped in from the hall.

"All right, class," she said. "Let's see how well you've been studying your vocab this week. That's right — pop quiz. It won't require any talking, thank you. You'll just need one sheet of paper and a pen."

Why had Maria thought her day couldn't get any worse? She was starting to think someone was out to get her.

CHAPTER 2

At lunch, Maria sat down and immediately pulled out her notes for her oral report, reading over them for the hundredth time. She was so nervous she felt like she had spiders in her stomach. She hated having to stand up in front of the class for anything.

Derek slid into the seat across from her, flipping his shaggy black hair, which was always falling in his eyes. He twirled a pen from one finger to the next.

"Oh, right," he said. "I forgot we had those reports next period."

"Please tell me you've got something prepared," Maria said. In truth, she envied the way he could approach everything so calmly. He always said that if something made you nervous, it just meant that you were thinking about it too hard.

"Yeah, don't worry. I'm going to do mine on my dad's shop."

Maria rolled her eyes.

"What?" Derek said. "It's *full* of local history. That shop has been in my family for, like, seventy-five years."

Derek's dad owned a store called Vic's Antiques. Derek always said he wished they'd change the name, since Vic referred to his great-grandfather, who'd passed away before Derek was even born. But Maria thought that made it the perfect name for an antique shop, especially one as full of the past as Vic's Antiques. There were all kinds of knick-knacks and oddities there. Like the seashell bracelet Maria was currently wearing, which had cost only three dollars after Derek's dad gave her the family discount.

"Hey, do you want to come visit Grandma Esme with me after school?" Maria said. Derek was one of the few people besides her who thought her grandmother was cool, not weird.

"Sorry, can't," he said, now twirling the pen so fast it was hard to tell which fingers he was using. "I promised my mom I'd help clean up the house before my great-aunt Luellen gets here."

"I forgot that she was coming this weekend. Well, I'll tell Grandma Esme you say hi."

"Yeah, thanks. You know I'd rather spend time at Grandma E.'s house than mine any day. Especially now, since I get the feeling from my mom that Aunt Luellen can be a little scary."

"Why is she here?"

"I'm not really sure. Dad said it was something about visiting an old friend, but I don't know who, because she's never lived in Florida before. She lives up in New York with the rest of the Overton side of the family."

"Weird," Maria said. "But I'm sure she's harmless."

"Fingers crossed," Derek said, stopping the pen mid-twirl in between his crossed fingers. "By the way," he said, "I heard you told Claire McCormick her face was ugly."

"Is that what's going around?" Maria smirked. "Well, I didn't use those words exactly, but I was definitely thinking them."

"Be careful around her," Derek warned. "That girl is frightening when she's mad."

"Claire McCormick doesn't scare me," Maria replied.

But she couldn't look Derek in the eye as she said it. He always knew when she wasn't telling the truth.

When the bus let Maria off at the end of Spinneret Street, she felt, as she always did, like she was stepping back in time. The houses on this street were some of the oldest in the city, although at this point they looked more run-down than historical. Still, Grandma Esme's house was like Grandma Esme — it had character. From the uneven wooden pillars holding up the front-porch roof to the stained-glass windows depicting the sun and the moon, the house was almost like a personal museum.

Maria loved it.

She knocked three times using the big brass knocker, then waited for the sound of her grandma coming to the door. After two whole minutes of nothing, she tried the handle. The door was unlocked.

"Grandma? Are you awake?" Maria called, stepping inside.

Something was wrong. That was immediately clear. The house was always a bit of a mess, but once you knew the pattern to the chaos (and the location of all the secret shelves and drawers), you could find anything you wanted without much trouble. Today, there was no pattern. It looked like a tornado had swept over a yard sale right here in the living room.

"Grandma?" Maria called more urgently.

"Who is it? Maria, is that you?"

Maria exhaled. Grandma Esme appeared in the doorway that led back to the kitchen, her black hair disheveled, her cat-eye glasses askew. She was clutching one of her silver whistles to her chest, and she had a light in her eyes like she'd just seen her own ghost.

"Yes, it's me, Grandma. Remember? I said I was coming over on Friday?"

"Oh," Esme said, but she still didn't smile. "Is it Friday already?"

"It is," Maria said patiently. She motioned to the heap of odds and ends piled on the living room carpet. "Did you lose something, Grandma? Do you want some help finding it?"

"What? Oh, no, dear. I mean, yes. Yes, I want your help. No, I haven't lost anything."

Maria walked over to her grandmother and held her hand. Sometimes, when Grandma Esme was feeling forgetful, you just needed to spend a quiet moment with her before the memories came back.

Grandma Esme looked down at their hands. Her eye lingered on her black spider ring, which always seemed to catch the light just right.

"It's the spiders," Esme said. "The spiders have returned."

"Which spiders? Do you mean real spiders?"

"Yes, real spiders," Grandma Esme said. "Very real. Too real."

Maria led Esme to the living room couch, guiding her around a few stray books and records along the way. Esme sat down and took a deep breath. This seemed to help.

"I'm so sorry, dear," Esme said. "I don't know where my head is. I suppose I must have lost track of the time."

"That's okay, Grandma. It's been a very long week."

"You too, huh? Is everything okay at school?"

"Yeah, it's fine," Maria said. She wasn't about to trouble her grandmother with Claire McCormick's nonsense.

"And where is our friend Derek today?"

"He had to help his mom clean. He said to tell you hello."

"Well, hello, Derek," Grandma Esme said, which made Maria smile.

"So what do you want to do today, Grandma? Do you want me to read to you?"

"A story would be nice," Grandma Esme said. "Nothing too scary, though. Not with the day I'm having."

Maria looked at the pile on the floor behind her, scanning the books that had been scattered about, hoping there might be one she hadn't read before.

A piece of yellowed paper caught her eye, buried beneath a glass flower vase that had been etched with spiderwebs. Maria carefully moved the vase and picked up the paper. It looked like an old movie poster, with a painting of a man in a billowy black cape and a woman in a star-speckled shawl, her hand disappearing into the mane of a lion that was as big as a horse. The lion was smiling, and its smile revealed four very sharp teeth. Big, blocky letters proclaimed THE AMAZING ARTURO AND ESMERELDA THE MAGNIFICENT: A DAZZLING DOUBLE ACT OF MAGIC AND DARING! So Grandma Esme's stories were true after all.

"Grandma, was this really you?" Maria asked, handing her grandmother the poster and pointing.

Esme adjusted her glasses and squinted, and it was like her eyes finally came into focus. Maria knew that look. The memories were back. "Ah, yes, Maria, that was really me. Arturo and I were childhood friends, you know, connected at the hip. A bit like you and Derek, though perhaps not as well-behaved. Of the three of us, Arturo was the true performer. Cocoa and I were just along for the ride."

"Cocoa?" Maria laughed. "Was that the lion's name?"

"It was. I gave him the choice of a few names, and that was his favorite."

Esme was smiling, but she looked wistful, too. Maria knew a little about her grandmother's childhood from her mom — that she'd been born in Europe, and had traveled the world after being forced to leave her family — but even her mom didn't know that much. Maria's dad had never talked about it back when he was alive.

Maria read the small print at the bottom of the poster. It looked like her grandmother's double act had been part of the Rimbaud Brothers traveling circus. A circus, the poster said, that had toured Europe seventy years ago. That couldn't be right . . . could it? There was no way her grandmother was that old. Her hair hadn't even begun to turn gray, for one thing.

"Arturo gave me this ring, you know," Esme said. "I wear it in his memory."

"What happened to him?" Maria asked.

Esme's eyes grew wide and wild. She worried the silver whistle in her hand, as if she were trying to polish it with her fingers.

"The *other* spiders," she whispered. "The other spiders got him. And they are after me, too, Maria. They are after my ring."

Maria's throat squeezed shut, like it had during her oral report that afternoon. It wasn't uncommon for Grandma Esme to sound paranoid. She'd often warned

Maria about "lurking enemies" and the best ways to stay hidden, and Maria had always assumed these warnings were leftover relics from her mysterious childhood. Maybe Esme's own parents had used those same words when Esme had been forced to leave them. But Grandma Esme had never gone so far as to suggest that the lurking enemies were *spiders*. In fact, she'd always told Maria that the spiders were her friends.

"Grandma, I think maybe we'd better take an afternoon nap —"

"No, listen to me, Maria. I am not tired, I am not joking, and I most certainly am not confused." She held out the whistle in her hand and shook it. "Do you see this? Do you? There is a reason I used this whistle to speak with Cocoa, when other lion tamers spoke with their whips. You cannot truly command a lion, Maria. You can give, and you can ask, and you can earn his respect. The lion tamer who uses a whip may find it easier to make an obedient animal, but he will never make a friend. And only a friend will help you in the end."

"I don't understand, Grandma. Are we talking about Derek?"

"The spiders, Maria! We are talking about the spiders. People with gifts like ours must always choose between doing what is right and what is easy. You must *promise me* that will you do what is right."

Maria wanted to ask, "What gifts do I have?"

But Esme had said "promise me" in a voice so commanding it was scary. So Maria said, "I promise," and left it at that.

Esme nodded, her mouth a resolute line.

"Good." She slipped the whistle into her pocket and took another deep breath. Then she smiled. "Now, if you could just help me find my kettle in all this rubble, we can have a cup of tea and enjoy that story."

Maria left to walk home at half past four, allowing herself more time than she needed before it got dark. The rest of her visit had been calm enough, with no more strange warnings and Grandma Esme in good humor. They'd picked mint leaves from Esme's garden for the tea, and then Maria had read aloud from a book of fairy tales — a story about a princess who, with the help of woodland creatures, defeats an evil shadow queen. Finally, they'd listened to old records on Esme's gramophone.

But through it all, Maria couldn't shake the image of her grandmother's haunted eyes as she claimed that the spiders were out to get her, warning Maria of the choice that lay ahead.

For the first time in Maria's life, believing in stories felt like a dangerous thing.

CHAPTER 3

The weekend went by as weekends normally did, with Rafi outside collecting rocks and insects from the creek, and Maria inside, tucked into her window seat with a book.

Her mother used to beg her to spend more time out in the sun, but she finally stopped after Maria pointed out that she never tried to make Rafi come in and read.

Maria spent Saturday night sewing the purple star patch onto her paisley shirt. It didn't look as good as new, but then, it hadn't been new when Maria had bought it. Grandma Esme always said that Maria's personal touches made her clothes *better* than new, but she was the only one who seemed to think so.

On Sunday, while she was cleaning her room as part of her weekly chores, Maria was alarmed to find a large cobweb blooming in the back of her closet. There didn't appear to be any spiders left on it, so she didn't hesitate to grab a broom and swat it down. She checked to make sure it hadn't gotten onto any of her clothes. The last thing she needed was for Claire to find something else on her shirt the next day.

The cobweb also reminded Maria of her afternoon with her grandmother. She hoped that had been a one-time incident, but decided she had better tell her mother about it, just in case. At dinner, she said, "Mom, Grandma Esme was acting kind of strange on Friday."

"Stranger than usual?" Rafi said, and Maria glared at him.

"Strange how?" Mom asked.

"I don't know. She just seemed . . . scared. Like she really thought something was out to get her." Maria didn't specify that Esme had said *spiders* were out to get her. That felt like telling on her grandmother, somehow. And she hated to give Mom and Rafi one more reason to think Grandma Esme was crazy.

"That's just how it is when you get to be Grandma Esme's age," Mom said. "Especially when it gets late in the day, and the sun goes down. Something chemical happens in your brain."

"Like a zombie?" Rafi said.

"No, zombies *eat* brains," Maria said, rolling her eyes. "Plus, the sun was still out when I was there. Mom, can you please just check on her?"

Maria's mom scrunched her eyebrows together like she did when Maria tried to explain the plot of one of her books. It was the same look she got when she was paying the bills. Finally, she said, "Of course I will, *mija*. I'll swing by her house before I pick you guys up tomorrow."

Rafi was quick to protest. "But, Mom, Rob asked if I could come over tomorrow. They're getting a new waterslide put in this weekend, and it's supposed to be finished by the time school's out."

"Isn't it a little cold to be swimming?"

"Nah. We were in the pool last weekend and it was fine."

"Maybe I'd better call Rob's father and make sure it's okay that you keep coming over."

"He already said it was," Rafi whined. "He said I was welcome anytime."

"I'll call him after dinner," Mom said firmly.

Maria didn't understand how Rafi could think about waterslides when she'd just said their grandmother wasn't doing well. Not even Derek was that carefree.

On the way back to her room, Maria discovered another large, abandoned spiderweb, this one strung up between the ceiling and the wall of the hallway. She shivered.

"Rafi!" she called. "Rafi, come look at this."

"What is it now?"

"Have you been leaving the back door open when you go outside? This is the second spiderweb I've found today."

"Well, it's not my fault. I didn't leave the door open. Maybe the spiders at Grandma Esme's house rode here inside your book bag. Did you think of that?"

"Fine, be that way," Maria said, leaving him in the hall and all but slamming the door behind her. She knew she wasn't really that mad at her brother, but it was like her anger was getting wrapped up inside her fear, and the two were becoming a tangled black knot that filled her head. If it was a coincidence that these webs were appearing now, after what Grandma Esme had said about the spiders returning, it was the worst coincidence in the history of coincidences.

Still, Maria hoped that it *was* a coincidence. The spiders had no *reason* to be here.

Right?

When Maria got to her seat in English, Claire was already at her desk smiling brightly, as if it weren't first thing on a Monday morning. Maria got nervous when Claire McCormick smiled. Her smile showed too many teeth, like a lion's.

"Hey, Maria. How was your weekend?" Claire asked through that smile.

"Fine," Maria said carefully.

"I'm so glad to hear that." It was almost convincing.

Was it possible Claire had been the one behind the cobwebs in her house? Maybe she'd planted spiders on Rob, counting on Rob to pass them accidentally to Rafi, who had brought them into the house without realizing it. But that was ridiculous. Maria was starting to sound as paranoid as Grandma Esme. Claire wasn't some villain in a fairy tale. She was just a girl in Maria's English class.

As soon as the bell rang, Ms. Wainscott began passing back their vocab quizzes from Friday. When Maria got hers, she was relieved to see that she had gotten all ten of the words right. She'd almost blanked on the definition of *disputatious*, until finally she'd realized it looked a lot like *dispute*.

"Wow, Maria, you're so smart. I *wish* I was as *smart* as you," Claire said, looking over Maria's shoulder. The sarcasm in Claire's voice was slick and dark, like oil. Everyone laughed as if Claire had said something clever. Maria's hand went self-consciously to the purple star on her sleeve, like maybe she could hide it before Claire noticed that, too.

"I told you not to mess with her," Derek said at lunch. He'd already finished his peanut-butter-and-jelly sandwich, and now he passed a big silver dollar back and forth between his hands. At times, it vanished from sight completely.

"She started it," Maria said, shrugging. She stared down into the beefaroni and orange slices that lay untouched on her tray. It was kind of sickening how they were almost the same color. "I keep thinking I just need to be mean right back. Let her see how it feels."

"Oh, yeah, that's a fantastic idea." Somehow Derek managed to sound kind even when he was teasing her — the opposite of Claire, who sounded mean even when she gave Maria a compliment. "Just talk to Ms. What's-Her-Name about it. I'm sure if she knew, she'd at least put Claire in a different seat."

For Derek, every problem in the world could be solved by talking it out. But Maria wasn't Derek. As she'd tried to explain, if she told on Claire, Claire would just get back at her in other ways, likely much worse than her usual teasing.

"So how is your aunt?" Maria asked, very much wanting to change the subject.

"Great-aunt. And fine," Derek said. "I mean, you can tell she's from New York. She's very fancy and she never, ever laughs, not even when my dad did that thing where he acts like he's going to shake your hand and then pulls a coin out of your ear. But she's nice enough. She liked it when I showed her the shop."

"Oh, I almost forgot — Grandma Esme says hello."

"Hello, Grandma Esme," Derek replied, which was exactly the right response.

"I found this old poster that proves all her circus stories are true. It showed her and the lion, just like she always says."

"Wow, really? I bet my dad would love to have that for the shop."

"Well, he can't have it — it's Grandma Esme's." This came out more forceful than Maria meant it to. Derek's eyes widened, and he stopped passing the coin, but the thing about Derek was that he never took anything personally.

"My bad. You know I just meant it sounds cool, right?"

"Yeah, I know. I'm sorry," Maria said. "Grandma Esme was just a little out of it on Friday, so I've been a little out of it since. This thing with Claire definitely isn't helping."

"Does *this* help?" Derek asked, cupping his hands as if he were holding them over a fire. Maria didn't understand what he was doing at first, until suddenly she realized the silver dollar was in her hands, impossibly.

"How did you do that?" Maria asked, amazed.

Derek grinned.

"You really want to know how I did it?"

"Yes."

"It's easy," Derek said. He leaned in like he was going to whisper the answer in her ear. Always the performer, just like his dad.

"The secret," he told her, "is practice."

When Maria went to get her books at the end of the day, there was a terrible surprise waiting for her at her locker. She didn't see it at first because there was a crowd of people in the way. She figured they must be waiting for that eighth-grade girl Kim Thomas, who seemed to have even more fans than Claire. But no, she realized. They were staring at her locker, on which duct tape, stickers, and even a few cloth patches had been plastered so thick she couldn't see an inch of the gray metal beneath.

Her face burned as she pushed through the crowd and tried to peel the junk off. No one was rude enough to laugh at her. But none of them moved to help her, either.

Of course this had been Claire's doing — the duct tape alone was all it took to know that — but Maria would have a hard time proving it to her teachers.

It took Maria so long to collect her things, she was sure her mother would be outside worrying when she got to the pick-up area. But not only was her mom not outside, she didn't arrive after five or fifteen minutes, either.

Soon, Maria was one of only a handful of students left waiting for their parents. The other kids all looked like they were used to this. One boy had pulled out a deck of cards, and he and his friends were settling down to play without anyone having to explain the rules. But Maria's mother always arrived on time. The fact that she wasn't here could only mean something bad.

Just as Maria was thinking she should either walk home or else call her mom from the front office, the school secretary, Ms. Vinita, came shuffling outside. Her eyes darted around frantically until they landed on Maria.

"Oh, honey," she said, hurrying over with her arms outstretched. Maria could almost predict what was going to come next, word for word, as if she'd heard it all in a dream. She let Ms. Vinita hug her, knowing that it was as much for the older woman to feel better as it was for Maria. "I'm so sorry," Ms. Vinita said, and the words sounded odd in her gruff voice, which more often could be heard doling out tardies and unexcused absences. "It's your grandmother. She's — well, she's . . . Your mother is still there. At her house. She wondered if you would feel okay to walk there by yourself."

Maria nodded.

"Okay, then," Ms. Vinita said, and that was the closest she could get to a good-bye. She turned to go back to the front office, while Maria walked, and then jogged, and then ran all the way to her grandmother's house.

CHAPTER 4

The air was different on Spinneret Street.

It was thinner somehow, as if Maria were at the top of a tall mountain and couldn't get enough oxygen into her lungs. Maybe that was because she'd just run twenty blocks, and now her legs burned and her breath came in deep gasps. Or maybe it was because the gray clouds swirling overhead were filling the air with moisture, threatening rain.

There was an ambulance in her grandmother's driveway, and Maria felt a sudden swell of hope that pulled her forward. Ms. Vinita had gotten it wrong. Or maybe she hadn't said *dead* because Esme wasn't dead at all. Maria ran through her grandmother's front door like it was the finish line of a race.

"Grandma Esme?" she called.

Maria sprinted into the living room, convinced she would find her grandmother there waiting for her. But sitting amid the scattered wreckage from Friday was her mother, looking like she'd just woken up from a nap and had no idea where she was. Maria knew immediately: There hadn't been a mistake.

Grandma Esme was really gone.

Maria went and sat down in the rubble next to her mom, who put her arm automatically around Maria's shoulder. Maria took off her glasses and wiped them on her sleeve.

"I'm so sorry, sweetie," her mother said. It was strange the way everyone kept apologizing to *her*, as if she were the one who had died.

Two EMTs, a man and a woman, came out from the kitchen, and Maria nearly jumped out of her skin. She'd already forgotten about the ambulance in the driveway.

The man nodded somberly in Maria's direction, then turned to her mom.

"Well, Ms. Lopez, I think that's everything."

Mom didn't even bother getting up from the ground. She just said "Thank you. I guess I'll call if I have any questions," and the man nodded again before he and the woman left.

Maria waited until she'd heard the front door click shut, then she said, "What happened?" Her voice was soft and scratchy from crying.

"Where to start?" Mom sighed. "Well, I came to check on Grandma Esme, just like I said I would. She wasn't coming to the door when I knocked, but she'd left it unlocked, so I popped my head in for a quick hello." Maria remembered that her grandmother had left the door unlocked on Friday, too. She had been forgetting more and more of the little things lately. "She still wasn't responding when I called, so finally I came back to the kitchen, and . . . Oh, Maria." She leaned her head on Maria's shoulder and cried.

Maria had seen her mother this emotional once before, but that was years ago. From the little she remembered, that time had been much worse. That was the time when the man from the army had shown up at their door, and said that her dad wouldn't be coming home after all.

"And she was already . . . *gone?*" Maria found that she couldn't bring herself to say the word *dead*, either. It was too real, too final. The word *gone* could just as easily mean that Grandma Esme was at the grocery store.

"Actually, no," Mom said. Maria gulped. "No, I found her right after she'd collapsed. But it was very peaceful. The EMTs said it was a heart attack, but she didn't seem to be in any pain. She sounded like she was ready to go, Maria. She led a very full and happy life, you know."

"Wait — you talked to her?" Maria said.

Her mother frowned. "Only a little."

"What did she say?"

Her mother sat up, then re-crossed her feet. She seemed to be stalling, as if she hadn't wanted the conversation to take this turn.

"Maria, your grandmother has been so confused these past few months —"

"Mom, what did she say?" Maria repeated anxiously.

"Oh, well, you know how she always was with spiders."

Maria felt goose bumps on her arms and legs. On Friday, her grandmother had warned her that the spiders were after her. Three days later, she had died, and with her last words she'd tried to warn her mother, too.

"There was one strange thing, though," her mom continued. She turned to face Maria, to watch her reaction. "She said she had left you something. She said it was in the seashelf. Does that word mean anything to you?"

It did. It meant a lot to her, in fact.

Once, years ago, Maria and Rafi had been playing hide-and-seek. They'd been at the beach all day with Mom, but Mom had dropped them off at Grandma Esme's so she could have a girls' night out. Grandma Esme's house wasn't big, and there weren't many good hiding places. But Maria had snuck into Grandma Esme's room and crawled under the bed, sure that Rafi wouldn't find her there. When he'd called, "Come out, come out, wherever you are," she'd felt the peculiar thrill of knowing that someone was looking for her. That there was nothing she could do now but wait and hope she'd chosen the right hiding spot.

Then, lying on her stomach, she'd spied a strange crack running through the wooden bedpost by her face. She'd reached out to touch it and let out a little gasp when a whole chunk of the wood came off in her hand. It hadn't been a crack at all, but the opening of a small shelf hidden right into the bedpost. This wasn't the first time Maria had come across a false door or a secret compartment in Grandma Esme's house. Once, in a hidden drawer under the bathroom sink, she'd found an old whistle with an anchor painted on the side. But each new space was like a delicious new secret. Maria wondered if even Grandma Esme knew about them all.

There hadn't been anything on the shelf under the bed when Maria had first discovered it. But it looked so empty and inviting, it gave Maria an idea. She reached into her pocket and palmed a seashell she'd found in a tide pool that morning. She set it on the shelf and replaced the wooden door.

"Got you!" Rafi had called hardly a second later, and Maria had banged her head on the bed frame in surprise.

The next time Maria had come over to Grandma Esme's house, she'd stolen away under the bed to see if the seashell was still there. She'd opened the compartment quickly, unable to bear the suspense. The seashell was gone, but in its place was a silver pendant necklace with a purple stone at the end. Underneath the necklace was a note that read: *Thank you for finding me!* It was signed, *The Seashelf.*

Maria and Grandma Esme had exchanged many presents like that — an origami crane for a spun yarn bracelet, a poem for a mood ring — but not so much in the past two years. Maria still wore the pendant necklace sometimes.

Now Maria turned to her mom, who clearly thought Grandma Esme had been out of her mind when she'd mentioned the seashelf.

"I know where she means," Maria said, standing up. "I'll go check it and be right back." She wanted to see what was there alone. She needed a moment by herself.

Maria got down on her hands and knees and crawled under Grandma Esme's bed. She was almost too big to fit all the way.

She removed the false piece of the bedpost and found a brown wooden box. It was not a perfect cube, which made it look handmade. Maria opened the top and came face-to-face with the black spider ring her grandmother always wore. The box trembled in her hands. That the ring was here, in a box on the seashelf, meant that Grandma Esme had taken it off sometime *before* her heart attack. *If* a heart attack was what she'd had, which Maria was seriously starting to doubt.

Turning the box over, Maria discovered a second hinge on the back — the bottom of the box must open, too. She was just about to check when her mother's voice beside the bed made her jump. It was the game of hide-and-seek all over again.

"What is it, Maria? What did she leave you?"

"It's her spider ring. The one she always wore."

Maria crawled out from under the bed. Mom's face was stuck somewhere between a smile and a frown, as if she wasn't sure how she felt about this gift. As a park ranger, Mom didn't have the same fear of spiders that Maria did, but she had always thought Grandma Esme's fascination with them bordered on the unhealthy.

"Well, that was . . . very nice of her," she managed.

Maria decided she would check the other side of the box later, at home.

"We need to go pick up your brother," Mom said. "I just called Rob's dad and told him what happened. I'm sure your brother is going to be very upset."

Maria imagined her brother reaching the bottom of the waterslide — imagined Rob's dad telling him to hop out of the pool and come inside for a second. That was always the way with bad news, it seemed: It came out of nowhere, before you were ready for it.

"Oh, *mija*-oh-my-a," Mom said, pulling Maria into a hug. Maria couldn't help it. She'd started crying again.

That night, Maria's mom ordered a pizza, and she, Maria, and Rafi sat in the living room not saying much. They'd put on a movie — something funny about a family of tractors who could talk and wanted to move from the farm to the big city — but none of them was really watching it. Rafi kept saying things that started with, "Remember that time when Grandma Esme . . ." But

Maria wasn't in the mood to reminisce with him. Just for tonight, she wanted to keep her memories to herself.

She must have fallen asleep on the couch at some point, and her mother must have carried her back to her room. At least, when she woke up in her bed, she couldn't think of how else she'd gotten there. Wondering what time it was, Maria reached for her glasses on her bedside table, but instead her hand closed around the box with the ring. She couldn't feel her glasses anywhere.

Without her glasses, Maria's vision was terrible. Her eye doctor had said she was legally blind, but Grandma Esme had always argued that Maria could see everything that mattered.

Maria clutched the ring box to her chest, missing Grandma Esme more than ever. She opened the top and removed the spider ring. She had seen it so many times before, she could almost picture it as she slipped it onto her finger. But the ring in her head was inseparable from its place on Grandma Esme's hand. This ring, surprisingly, fit Maria's finger exactly. She wanted to get a closer look, but she didn't dare try to make her way to the living room in the dark without her glasses.

If only my glasses would come to me, she thought.

No sooner had she thought this than a strange rustling sound, like the *swish* of two hands rubbing together in the cold, reached her ears. She sat up higher in her bed, and after a tense few moments in which she was certain someone was in the room with her, she suddenly felt a small weight on her legs.

She reached out, trembling, and when her fingers closed around her glasses, she wasn't sure whether to feel relieved or terrified.

"Who's there?" she whispered, scrambling to put on her glasses. She still couldn't make out much in the darkness, but, blinking, she thought she saw *something* moving, like a cascade of shadows pouring in from the hall.

She leaned over and turned on her bedside lamp, then let out a sudden yip. A tiny brown spider with long, thin legs was scurrying down the lampshade. It wasn't alone.

There were brown spiders everywhere, covering her bedspread, her table, her walls. The shock of it paralyzed her. It was as if her mind was too busy taking in the sight to remind her to scream for help.

And yet, even as she watched, the spiders were moving away from her. A small circle of them were skittering from the spot on her lap where her glasses had been.

Her mind came unstuck. She found her voice.

"Did you . . . did you just bring me my glasses?" she whispered to the room.

The spiders stopped in their tracks. They turned to face her.

"Can you understand me?" she said. She supposed she should have started with that one.

If the spiders could understand her, they couldn't seem to reply. But they were standing there still, in rapt attention. And really, that was reply enough.

"I'm sorry if the light scared you," Maria said. "But to be fair, you scared me first."

The spiders continued to stare at her.

"All right, I *did* wish for the glasses to come to me. So . . . what I mean to say is, thank you."

At this, the spiders seemed — well, *pleased*. They resumed their march out of Maria's room, but not before they had formed a proud sort of pattern on Maria's wall, like two lines dancing in and around each other. And if, like Maria, they were still a little scared, at least they didn't seem to be hurrying so much.

When the last of the spiders had gone, Maria breathed deeply and willed her heartbeat to slow. Whatever she'd told them, she'd truly been terrified. If these were the spiders her grandmother had warned her about, she may have been lucky to escape with her life. Had the ring protected her?

Maria looked down at her hand. She hadn't imagined it; the ring really did fit her perfectly.

Hoping for some further clue, Maria reached for the ring box and brought it up to her eyes. The box was a rich brown wood that had been polished unevenly. Four untidy letters had been scratched into the bottom:

Maria had no idea what the letters meant, and she paused, feeling suddenly like she was prying into a secret that wasn't hers to know. But her grandmother had wanted her to have this ring and this box. Whatever was inside, it belonged to her now.

Slowly, fearfully, she pried open the bottom lid. A piece of paper fell out, folded into the shape of a crane just like the one Maria had left Grandma Esme years ago. When Maria unfolded it, she found a note written in her grandmother's cursive.

The spiders are your friends, the first line read. And underneath that:

Do not abuse their friendship.

CHAPTER 5

News of Grandma Esme's death traveled fast, and the next day saw an almost constant parade of visitors bearing casseroles and desserts. Rob and Claire's mom came by with banana pudding. A bouquet of flowers arrived with a note from Derek's parents. And a group of fellow park rangers from Falling Waters brought a whole cooked turkey, along with a collection they'd taken up to help pay for the funeral.

All in all, the day felt so out of the ordinary that it only furthered Maria's feeling that none of it was really happening.

It wasn't until Derek came over around three thirty that everything finally started to sink in.

"Maria, Derek's here," Rafi called from the front door. Her brother had been antsy all day, happy at first to get to stay home from school, but then, when Mom had said he couldn't play outside, increasingly rambunctious.

Derek had been to Maria's house enough times that he usually didn't have a problem walking right in (and going straight for the refrigerator). Today, he stood on the doormat, looking in every direction but straight ahead and fidgeting absently with a single yellow flower.

"Hi," Maria said, shooting her brother a look to let him know he could leave now. Rafi shrugged and went to join Mom in the kitchen.

"Hi," Derek said.

"Is that for me?" Maria nodded to the flower in Derek's hands.

"What? Oh, yeah." He seemed to have forgotten that he was holding a flower at all, but now he handed it to Maria with a flourish. "Well, you and your family. Mom said yellow means hope. And friendship."

"Thanks."

"Also, I took notes for you in history. We started on the Civil War."

"Thanks."

Maria racked her brain for the right thing to say. Something like, "Grandma Esme really liked you," or maybe, "Thanks for always being so nice." She knew Derek would have no problem saying something like that if their roles were reversed. What she finally said, in a breathless whisper, was, "Do you want to see what Grandma Esme left me?"

Derek smiled, nodded, and followed her inside. Mom always made Maria keep her door open when she had friends over, but today Maria bent the rule, leaving it open only a crack.

She went to her dresser and pulled out the second drawer. She reached into the back and removed the wooden box. She opened it toward Derek.

"Whoa," he said, leaning in until his face was almost right next to it. "That's the one she always wore, right?"

"Yup. She left it for me in one of our secret hiding places. Don't you think it's weird that she took it off like that? Almost like she knew something was going to happen to her."

Derek gave her a funny look. "You don't think . . . I mean, my mom said it was a heart attack . . ."

"Well, that's what the ambulance people said. But Mom said when she got there, Grandma Esme was still awake. She even talked to her. Does that sound like a person who's having a heart attack? And plus, she said the thing about the spiders again. The same stuff she was saying to me on Friday."

Her theory seemed to upset Derek immensely.

"You really think someone would *hurt* your grandma?" he asked.

"No. No, not really," she said, if only to make him feel better. "But there's something else. When I put the ring on last night, I'm pretty sure that — Well, it's going to sound crazy, but I'm pretty sure that it made the spiders in my house *listen* to me."

Now Derek had a very different look on his face. His right eyebrow arched up higher than the left, and his mouth turned down in a skeptical line.

"I'm serious, Derek. My glasses were in the living room, and I wished that they would come to me. And the spiders, well — they *brought* them."

"And you saw this happen without your glasses on?"

"No. Not exactly. I mean, I heard them, and then I sort of talked to them, and then I saw them leave. Basically."

"Right."

"Oh, and there was this note from Grandma Esme." She opened the bottom of the box and showed him the cryptic letter — the one she was blaming for her nightmare last night about sitting at a table with seven spiders and playing a game of cards. In the nightmare, she'd thought it was funny that there were seven spiders instead of eight. Then she'd realized that *she* was the eighth spider. She'd woken up itching.

Derek read the note. If anything, his eyebrow only shot higher.

"Okay, yeah, so this is a little weird. But, Maria — and I mean this in the nicest possible way, because I loved your grandma, you know that — Grandma Esme has been a little *confused* lately. My mom said maybe she had dementia or the other thing, old-timer's."

"Alzheimer's," Maria said sharply. "And, Derek, she was scared. She wasn't crazy."

"I didn't say 'crazy.' I said 'confused.'"

"You believe in magic, don't you?"

"What? What do you mean?"

"I mean like the coin, and the pen, and all that stuff. You do it because you believe in magic, right? Well, what if this ring is magic, too?"

"Maria, those are all magic *tricks*. 'Tricks' is the key word. You want me to tell you how I did the coin trick for real? Because I'll tell you. I just —"

"No, I don't want to know," Maria said, cutting him off and putting her fingers in her ears. "La la la," she said.

Derek gave up then, his shoulders slumping like he'd just bowled a gutter ball.

"Tell you what," he said, gently pulling her hands from her ears. "How about you bring the ring by my dad's shop? Maybe he'll be able to tell us something about it. He's got all those appraisal books and stuff. And if it's got powers — I mean, if it's *rumored* to have powers — he'll be the one to know."

Derek's dad *did* know an awful lot about antiques. He'd even shown Maria a collection of old rings once and told her what some of the symbols meant. But Maria wasn't sure she was ready to tell anyone else about the ring. Her grandmother hadn't just left it for her; she'd left it for her in a secret box on a secret shelf. There had to be a reason for all that secrecy.

"The funeral is on Thursday," Maria said. "And tomorrow, Mom and I are going back to her house to sort through her stuff. Maybe after everything is done, I'll bring it by."

"Does that mean you won't be at school all week?"

Maria nodded. "Mom said I should go back on Friday. Give myself the day to catch up without too much pressure."

"Man. How will I survive lunch without you?"

Maria smiled. She knew that Derek was only being nice — any day she wasn't there, there were a ton of people who would want him at their lunch table. But still, it made her feel better just having a friend who wanted her to feel better.

"I don't know," Maria said. "I guess it's like a magic trick. The secret is practice."

. . .

The next day, Maria, Rafi, and Mom went back over to Spinneret Street. Mom had handled all the official business with the funeral home that morning — Maria couldn't bear to be there for that — but she needed help organizing and cleaning the house. It had been left to them in Grandma Esme's will, and Mom had hinted that her plan was to sell it. Maria was just waiting for her to say it outright so she could argue. The house was all but built out of memories. Every architectural imperfection and secret hideaway was another family story told in wood and concrete.

When she thought about it practically, Maria knew that her family could use the money. And their house was bigger than Grandma Esme's, so it didn't make sense for them to move. She just hated that she was being forced to think practically at a time like this.

Mom fiddled with the lock on the front door, as if she couldn't figure out how to work it. Finally, she said, "Huh," and pushed the door open. "I could have sworn we locked it when we left the other day."

Maria shivered. She was *sure* they'd locked it when they'd left on Monday.

And there was more amiss than the door. Mom and Rafi didn't seem to notice, but to Maria, the differences were obvious. There was still a large pile of stuff on the living room floor, and the cabinets and shelves were still teeming with books and bric-a-brac. But everything had been rearranged, just a little bit. Objects were in different orders or inches from where they had been.

"Someone's been here," Maria said.

"What? For real?" Rafi said, looking to Mom to confirm or deny this.

"Maria, stop scaring your brother. This is not the time for that kind of behavior."

"I'm not kidding," Maria argued. "They could still be in the house *right now*. We shouldn't be here."

Rafi grabbed Mom's hand, looking like he might cry, but Maria was too scared herself to enjoy that fact.

"That's enough, young lady," Mom said, disappointment and worry competing on her face. "Both of you, outside. Right now. I'll come get you in a minute. Hopefully you'll be ready to behave a little more maturely then."

Mom ushered them out over Maria's protests. Maria and Rafi stood there in the little front yard, their eyes glued to the door. Every second that went by was another second in which Maria was convinced something terrible was happening to her mother. What if the spiders were in there wrapping her up in a web right now? Maria wished she'd worn the spider ring today. Maybe then she could ask the spiders to leave Mom alone, please.

Finally, the front door opened and Mom came out. Maria and Rafi exhaled together.

"Okay, guys, all clear. Now can I count on you two to be helpful today and work together? We've got a lot to do." Mom said this to both of them, but she was especially watching Maria.

"Yes, ma'am," Maria said.

As soon as she was back in the house, though, she went straight for Grandma Esme's bedroom and peeked under the bed. Sure enough, the door to the seashelf had been removed. Maria found it all the way across the room, as if it had been flung there in frustration. Someone definitely had been here since Monday. And whoever it was, Maria had a pretty good idea what they'd been looking for.

"What are you doing in here?" Rafi stood in the

doorway. He eyed the piece of wood in Maria's hand with a mixture of fear and suspicion.

"None of your business," Maria said.

"Mom said we're supposed to work together."

"Trust me, Rafi — you don't want to work with me. The less you know about what I'm doing, the safer it is for you."

Rafi rolled his eyes. "You're just trying to scare me again."

"Believe what you want. But don't come crying to me when the spiders . . ."

"What? When the spiders what?"

But Maria couldn't speak. Her throat was closing up again, the way it always did when she was terrified. She'd been in such a hurry to check the seashelf, she hadn't noticed the spiderweb stretching over the inside of the doorway. Now a fat black spider with a bright red spot was scuttling down that web, lowering itself right into the air above Rafi.

Rafi could see the fear in Maria's eyes, but he didn't turn or run. Instead, he scoffed.

"Let me guess, when the spiders *come and get me?* Maybe when I'm asleep?"

In the second before the spider landed on Rafi, Maria reached out and grabbed her brother's hand. She pulled him so hard they both fell backward, and he let out a yell of surprise that Maria matched with a scream of her own.

"What in the world is going on back here?" Maria's mom rounded the corner to the room so fast she nearly collided with the black spider, which dangled in the air a few feet above the ground. But she recoiled just in time, sizing up the situation and reaching immediately for her foot. Shoe in hand, she pulled back her arm to strike.

"No, Mom, don't!" Maria shouted.

"Maria, it's a black widow. See the little red hour-glass on its belly? That's because when it bites you, you can go thirty minutes before you feel it, and then you don't have much time left. One bite from that thing and I'd have to take you to Dr. Gutierrez right away."

"I don't care. Don't hurt it," Maria pleaded.

"She's right," Rafi said. He was breathing heavily beside her. "Grandma Esme always said we shouldn't hurt the spiders."

Their mom looked at them as if she wanted to disagree. Or maybe she was just processing the fact that, for once, she was the one who wanted to kill a little creature, and Maria was the one who was sticking up for it. Unless Maria was crazy, the black widow spider had paused as well, like maybe it knew Maria held its fate in her hands.

"All right," Maria's mom said at last. "But if either of you starts feeling sick, we're headed to the doctor. Now I'll go get a jar from the kitchen, and we'll release this little guy in the woods at home. Both of you stay where you are until I get back."

The black widow spider had other ideas. As soon as Maria's mom disappeared down the hall, it turned to look at Maria and Rafi. Maria knew she wasn't crazy this time — the spider clearly moved its body around to face them. Then, so fast that Maria could hardly follow, it pulled itself back up to its web, then scurried into the corner of the ceiling and disappeared.

Maria exhaled.

"That was close. I hope we made the right call," she said.

Rafi stared at her as if she had just sprouted an extra set of eyes. Then he gave her a hug, jumped to his feet, and ran to the kitchen, leaving Maria to wonder whether her life would ever feel normal again.

CHAPTER 6

Maria was exhausted when she got home that evening.

Even ignoring the close call with the spider, cleaning Grandma Esme's house had been draining, physically and emotionally. Every single object had been just so heavy with history. But the funeral, which was happening first thing the next morning, promised to be more draining still. Maria wasn't sure she had it in her to put on a brave face in front of strangers.

On the bright side, Maria's mom had heard from Derek's parents that his whole family would be there, and that knowledge gave Maria courage.

Maria avoided her room for as long as she could that night. She reread a book that she'd left in the living room.

She asked her mom five times who was going to be at the church in the morning. She even offered to help her mom do the dishes from dinner, which was the exact moment when her mom guessed she was afraid to be alone.

But that wasn't the issue, or at least not all of it.

When Maria finally dragged her feet back to her bedroom, her eyes went straight for the box on her nightstand. She approached it slowly, as if she needed to sneak up on it.

Someone else knew about the ring's mysterious powers, and that someone may have killed her grandmother trying to get them. Maria herself still didn't know what those powers *were*, exactly. She had wanted her glasses, and the spiders had brought them. Did that mean the spiders could read her mind? Could she *command* the spiders, or just ask them politely for things? Were these regular spiders or magical ones?

Maria had read a book once about a groundskeeper who kept a very large spider as a pet, until it escaped into the woods and tried to eat people. If magical spider rings existed, maybe giant people-eating spiders did, too. Maybe Maria had control over them.

Her imagination was getting away from her again.

Derek was right. It probably hadn't been magic, but a magic *trick*. And not even the fun kind of trick — the kind that ended with *abracadabra*, *voilà*, or *ta-da*. This was the kind of trick like Claire McCormick's smile, the kind that made you confused about something important. This kind of trick preyed on people who wanted desperately to believe something, like the fact that magic and stories were real. What had Derek said? Grandma Esme was "confused"? Maybe Grandma Esme had believed too much in a magic trick, too.

Maria pulled the spider ring out of the box once more. She slipped it delicately on her finger. It really was a beautiful ring when you looked at it. The level of detail on the spider was so fine, down to its sharp pincers and tiny leg joints, it was as if it wasn't a carved stone at all, but a real spider that had calcified and been placed on a band. But it couldn't be a real spider. For one thing, this spider had six eyes, when Maria was almost positive that all spiders had eight.

Now that Maria looked at it, she thought she saw something on the underside of the spider's abdomen. A tiny clasp, if she wasn't mistaken. She tried to pry it open with her fingernails, and finally, the mechanism clicked, revealing a small container. It was hardly big enough to hold anything, and it was empty now, though Maria thought she saw the residue of a fine powder along the edges.

There was a name for rings like this that hid little containers. "Poison rings," Derek's dad had called them once. The idea was that old knights and kings would keep real poison in them, either for their enemies or else, if they were captured, for themselves. But more often, poison rings held medicine or mementos. A locket of hair or a whiff of perfume. Poison rings sometimes had another name, for that very reason. "Funeral rings," for the mourners left behind.

In spite of that name, Maria smiled.

Leave it to Grandma Esme to have a ring with a secret compartment.

"Are you okay, sweetie?" Mom said, appearing suddenly in her doorway. Maria realized she must have looked odd, sitting here admiring her ring.

"Yeah, just missing her," she said.

"I miss her, too," her mom said. She stared into the middle distance, as if she could see Grandma Esme there in the room with them. She shivered. "She was a real one-of-a-kind lady, your grandmother."

"Two-of-a-kind," Maria replied.

"Is that right?" Her mother's smile didn't quite reach her eyes. "Well, it's true you got her imagination. Your father had it, too."

"Really?"

"Does that surprise you?"

"Well, you just always say that Dad didn't like stories that much."

Maria's mother sat down on the edge of her bed.

"Oh, I said he wasn't a reader like you are, but he always liked stories. He used to say he was going to buy us one of those fishing boats in the gulf, and that we would all go on an adventure, to Japan and Australia and everywhere."

Maria liked the sound of a boat trip around the world. It was too bad her father wasn't here to make it come true.

"Who knows, maybe after we sell Grandma Esme's house, we can finally buy that boat after all. I've been thinking we could use a little more family adventure around here."

Maria wasn't sure if she *did* need any more adventure. It seemed to be finding her well enough already. Her feelings must have shown crystal clear on her face, because her mother backtracked and changed the subject.

"Do you have your clothes picked out for tomorrow? We need to leave around eight thirty so we can get to the church a little early."

"I'll put my clothes out," Maria said. She already knew she didn't have anything special to wear. She had one black dress and one green dress, which she alternated between for church and special occasions. The black dress might have been stylish once. The green dress looked like it had been a fir tree in a past life.

"All right, then. If you're sure you're okay . . ."

"I'm sure."

"Good night, sweetie."

"Good night, Mom."

Her mother leaned in for a hug, and then got up to go back to her room. Maria stopped her in the doorway.

"Mom?" she said.

"Yes, *mija*-oh-my-a?"

"Do you think Dad and Grandma Esme are together again?"

"Of course they are. And since I don't believe in stories, you know it's true."

This was exactly the right response.

When Maria turned out her light to go to sleep, she kept the spider ring on, deciding that this was a fitting way to keep Grandma Esme close tonight. Her black dress lay draped over her chair like she'd promised, its little quarter sleeves threatening to make Maria look like a Victorian baby doll the next day, when she wanted to appear sophisticated and somber. If only she'd thought to grab one of Grandma Esme's shawls. *Then* she would have looked like Esmerelda the Magnificent's granddaughter.

She closed her eyes and imagined the kind of dress she would buy if she had unlimited money. A sleek dress, elegant and mysterious. A dress that said, *Here is a girl who is not to be trifled with.*

As Maria lay there picturing her dress, the ring on her finger began to grow warm. Faster than she could think, she scrambled to slide the ring off her finger, removing it so forcefully that it flew and landed somewhere at her feet. The best thing to do was put it back in the box, she decided. Then she'd put the box back in her sock drawer, and then maybe push her dresser out into the hall.

When Maria turned on her light and picked up the ring box, she opened it wrong-side up and found the note from Grandma Esme staring her in the face.

The spiders are your friends. Do not abuse their friendship.

Were they her friends, or were they out to get her? Could they be both at once? Perhaps her grandmother really had been crazy after all.

Finally, Maria decided that if the spiders had wanted to get her, they easily could have done so while she was asleep last night. Boldly — or was it recklessly? — Maria put the ring back on her finger and said in a small voice, "I wish I had a beautiful dress to wear to Grandma Esme's funeral."

This time, she hardly flinched when she felt the ring heat up. And when the line of brown spiders came trickling in through the crack under her door, she greeted them with what she hoped was a convincing smile.

The spiders got to work at once. They swarmed and surrounded Maria's baby-doll dress, until she could hardly see the fabric underneath the cloud of moving legs.

"Be careful," Maria couldn't help saying, hoping that this wouldn't offend them. She could just imagine explaining to her mom why one of her two dresses was ruined. The problem with being a park ranger who didn't believe in stories was that sometimes even the truth was unbelievable.

The spiders didn't seem to be offended, though. If anything, they worked faster, some of them swinging from the chair on strands of cottony spider silk. Maria could even swear she heard the buzz of voices. But as soon as the word *voices* formed in her mind, the buzzing she thought she heard was gone.

At last the army of spiders began to break ranks, scurrying to leave in separate waves. When the final few stragglers completed their work and left, Maria felt the ring go cold.

From where she sat in her bed, she could already see that her dress had changed. She put one foot on the floor and then the other, crossing her room as fast as she could on her tiptoes.

When she got to the dress, she gasped.

Each shoulder strap of this old-but-new creation was formed from three strands of black fabric woven into a braid. When Maria touched it, the fabric felt different than it had before, like expensive silk, only softer, if that was possible. The body of the dress was made of the same rich fabric. Around the waistline, rows of shimmery sequin-like orbs crisscrossed until they met at a spiral in the back.

When Maria lifted the dress and looked at the chair beneath, she discovered the best detail of all: two sheer black gloves, each long enough to stretch past her elbow, with interlocking webs to match the pattern on the dress.

Maria could hardly believe her good fortune. She decided to try on the dress now, just in case this was a dream. She'd hate to wake up in the morning and realize she'd missed her chance to see how it looked on her.

She slipped her arms through the straps and put the gloves on second. She stood in front of her mirror and struck a commanding pose.

Dream or reality, Maria would cherish this sight forever. She looked strong. She looked beautiful. In the darkness, in this dress, she was Maria the Magnificent.

"Maria, wake up. It's after eight already."

Maria rubbed her eyes and sat up in bed. She'd been in the middle of the most wonderful dream, but now she couldn't remember a single detail except the feeling of happiness. She reached for her glasses and felt the surprising weight of the spider ring on her finger. She must have left it on all night.

Not entirely knowing why, Maria shuddered.

She got out of bed, meaning to head straight for the bathroom and the shower. But the black dress on her chair stopped her cold.

The elegant straps, the black, webbed gloves — they were really here. She hadn't imagined it.

Maria was so caught up in the wonder of the moment, a moment just like her dream, the feeling of pure happiness, that it wasn't until her mother called, "Maria, are you up?" that she came to her senses and understood what had happened.

She had wished for a dress, and now here it was. And it hadn't been chipmunks or bluebirds that had made it for her, either. It was spiders. It was like Maria was in some kind of fairy tale, only she wasn't the princess who fell asleep for centuries to be awoken by a prince. She was the shadow queen.

"Yes, Mom, I'm up," she said, before her mother could come in and find her like this. What was she supposed to do now? Her own black dress was missing, but she couldn't very well wear this brand-new gown — a gown that hadn't been made by humans — and expect her mother not to realize something was going on.

What had Grandma Esme always said when Maria asked her about her clothes? "I got this in Europe." Either that, or, just like the ring, "It was a gift from a friend."

The spiders are your friends.

So that was it, then. Grandma Esme's clothes had been made by spiders.

Maria set the dress and the gloves down and went through the motions of getting ready. Brushing her teeth, combing her hair. She was glad to have something so routine to do after discovering something so utterly strange. It helped her to pretend that this was just another day.

But it wasn't just another day, not by a long shot.

Grandma Esme was dead, and magic was real.

These were just two facts Maria would have to get used to.

PART TWO

THE MIRROR SPIDER

We are the spiders of the Order of Anansi.

We feast on the dreams of the lost and forgotten.

We seek our treasures in deep, dark places

And hide in the shadows until it's too late.

CHAPTER 7

Maria hadn't been to Grandma Esme's church in a long, long time. As far as she could tell, there wasn't any particular reason why Grandma Esme had gone to one church while Maria, Rafi, and Mom had always gone to another. Mom had once explained that the churches were "different denominations," but when Maria had asked what that meant, exactly, Mom had said, "It means your father was raised one way, and I was raised another."

Maria had let the subject drop.

Grandma Esme's church looked a little bit like Maria's school, with brown brick walls that stretched out instead of up, except for one tall steeple that stretched up quite a ways. The church had a lower level with long tunnels and passages — you could go down in the kitchen and come up behind the sanctuary, and if you weren't careful, you could hit your head on the loading doors that led into the parking lot. Maria sometimes wondered if the basement was the reason Grandma Esme had picked this church.

"Are we the first ones here?" Rafi said, pressing his nose against the car window as they pulled into the parking lot.

"No, look. I think that's the preacher's car." Mom nodded at a little white sedan parked all the way in the back.

They got out of the car and walked around to the front doors of the church. Maria still felt a bit self-conscious in her beautiful dress. It almost seemed too pretty to wear to a funeral, especially next to her mom's gray pantsuit and her brother's wrinkly blazer.

Her mother looked back at her and seemed to agree.

"I can't believe your grandmother had that sitting in her closet. It's a perfect fit."

"I know, right? I think maybe she bought it for my birthday or something," Maria lied.

"Right. Your birthday," her mom said skeptically. She tried the doors, and, finding them locked, knocked loudly three times.

After a moment, the doors swung inward, and a short, white-haired man who looked entirely too cheerful stood waiting to greet them.

"Ah, look at you," he said brightly, clapping his hands together. "Maria, I haven't seen you since you were this high. And, Rafael, you were just a baby."

"I go by Rafi now," Rafi mumbled.

"I don't believe we've met," Mom said, sticking out her hand for a handshake.

"You're right, of course," the man said, taking Mom's hand warmly in both of his. "I'm Winston Yarmuth, the pastor here. And you're Sofia Lopez. I've just heard so many wonderful things from Esmerelda, I feel like I already know all of you."

Mom smiled. "How can we help you set up, Mr. Yarmuth?"

"Help me? Oh, no, Ms. Lopez, everything is finished. Esmerelda had so many friends here. They all stayed late to help set up last night."

They followed Pastor Yarmuth into the sanctuary and saw immediately what he meant. There were flowers *everywhere*. On the pews, on the front podium, even in the windows. There had been a brief moment on the drive over when Maria wondered what would happen if no one came to the funeral but Derek's family and them. Grandma Esme always seemed to live such a solitary existence, and rarely talked to Maria about what she did when Maria wasn't there, unless it was to tell her stories about the past.

With nothing left to do but wait, Mom, Rafi, and Maria sat in the very front pew. Rafi borrowed Mom's phone and played a game that involved lining up pieces of fruit on a checkerboard. Maria pulled out a hymnal and turned to the back, where the stories behind many of the songs could be found.

Finally, around nine fifteen, people started to trickle in. Some people came as families, others by themselves, but all of them seemed to know one another. And all of them came first to Pastor Yarmuth, and then, after he pointed them out, to Maria's family. Mom made Rafi put the phone away and stand up, and the three of them had to give hugs to one person after another, all of whom said they had heard so many wonderful things from Esmerelda.

"Wow. I guess she was pretty popular, huh?" Rafi said, when at last the church looked to be filled to capacity. Maria had to agree.

With five minutes until the service began, Derek's family came hurrying through the doors. Derek's dad spotted them right away and headed up to say hello, though there weren't any more seats left in the front pew.

"Sorry we're late," Mr. Overton said. "Derek couldn't find his tie this morning, and then I took a wrong turn by the bypass."

Maria caught Derek's eye and raised her eyebrows. She was eager to tell him what had happened last night with the ring and the dress. But he only offered her a weak smile in return, as if the morning had been even more hectic than his dad was letting on.

Then Maria noticed the woman standing next to Derek. Tall, slender, and stunningly pretty, this had to be his great-aunt Luellen. She wore a black hat with a brim that swept diagonally across her forehead, all but covering the right side of her face. Her posture made her look sharp but casual at the same time, like a cursive *S*. She looked the way Maria imagined all women in New York did.

"You must be Maria," she said in a rich, smoky voice. She took Maria's hands in hers and squeezed. "I was so sorry to hear about your loss."

"Nice to meet you," Maria said, pulling her hands back to her sides. She understood now why Derek's mom had said Luellen was a little scary. But Derek's parents were still talking to Mom, and Rafi was listening in, clearly bored. Derek stared off into space. Maria couldn't decide whether or not he was avoiding her eyes. *Well, fine, then,* she thought.

"That's a beautiful dress you're wearing," Luellen said.

"Thank you. It was my grandmother's."

Luellen pinched the fabric of Maria's shoulder strap between her fingers. After an uncomfortably long moment, she leaned in and said, "You know, I actually saw your grandmother once, a long time ago. Did you know she used to travel with a famous circus?"

Maria didn't know what to say. Derek came out of whatever trance he'd been in, equally surprised. That was a relief, at least.

"You saw my grandma Esme do a show?"

"Oh, yes. Many years ago now, in a charming little village in Switzerland. I was there on business, and I was intrigued by an advertisement for the Amazing Arturo and Esmerelda the Magnificent. They were the headliners of the whole circus, you see. Your grandmother was the only lion tamer at that time — or since, as far as I know — who could control her beast with nothing but a whistle. Arturo, meanwhile, would do the most unbelievable things with just a handkerchief and a mirror. Their grand finale was to make the lion disappear. They really were quite extraordinary together. I'll never forget it."

Maria started to ask whether there had been any *other* animals involved in the act, but Pastor Yarmuth called the service to order then, and the Overtons had to make their way to the only pew still open, the very last one in the back.

Maria struggled to focus on Pastor Yarmuth's speech. With each new warm story he told, she only missed her grandmother more.

She stared up into the tall ceiling of the sanctuary. She could see past the wood beams to the place where all the walls of the church came together in a point, the inside of the steeple. She was surprised — and then not so surprised — to see that a swarm of spiders had gathered in the rafters, their webs like thick clouds from the sky beyond.

These weren't the black spiders with red hourglasses that meant your time was up. These were the brown spiders that had made Maria's dress. These were the spiders that had been Grandma Esme's friends. These were the spiders that had come to say good-bye.

Maria wished that she had worn her ring. She wanted to tell the spiders thank you.

The service itself was done in no time. It was the walk back to the car, and then the drive to the cemetery, that took forever.

The crowd at the gravesite was smaller than it had been at the church. Derek's family had taken him on to school, and many of the church members had gone their separate ways. But a smaller crowd still meant a lot of people.

Almost everyone here was crying. Mom wept quietly, her back held straight and her hands bunched in a knot. Even Rafi had tears in his eyes.

Maria didn't cry. She kept her composure. *A shadow queen is still a queen,* she thought.

Then, from behind a tree across the way, a moving shape caught Maria's eye. The shape was black and seemed human at first, but the more Maria watched it, the less human it seemed. One moment it looked like a distant grave; the next it just looked like the thin shadow of the tree. Maria squinted her eyes and stared, and for a second she was sure that yes, it was a person — a man in a black suit who was very tall and very thin — but as soon as she'd seen him, he'd disappeared again.

And then Maria was being ushered forward by her mother. She was supposed to throw a handful of dirt on Grandma Esme's grave. Maria hesitated. This felt like saying she agreed with the burial — that she wanted it to happen, or allowed it somehow. But she knew she'd start a fight if she refused to do it, so she picked up her handful of dirt and threw it in.

By the time she looked up, the man or the shadow was nowhere in sight.

CHAPTER 8

As a final sign of how upside down the day was, Rob was allowed to spend the night with Rafi, even though it was a school night.

When Maria answered the door, and Rob dashed straight back to Rafi's room with his overnight bag, Mr. McCormick handed Maria a bowl of banana pudding with an apologetic smile. Before she could say that they hadn't finished the first one, Mr. McCormick said, "Sorry about this. I guess Terry's *gone bananas* from all the party planning this week."

Maria laughed politely and thanked him for the pudding. She'd completely forgotten Claire's birthday party was the next day.

"Will we see you at our house tomorrow night?" Mr. McCormick said warmly.

"No, I —" She'd started to say that she hadn't been invited, since apparently he didn't know. She liked the idea of Claire getting in trouble with her parents. But now didn't seem like the time to shatter Mr. McCormick's image of his daughter, right when he'd done her family a kindness. "I just have so much going on this week. Helping my mom and all."

"Right, of course. Where are my manners? I'm so sorry about your grandmother."

Maria shrugged. She still didn't know how to respond when adults said this.

"Please tell your mother hello, and thanks again for putting up with Rob tonight. You call me if he gives you any trouble."

Mr. McCormick winked at her and headed back to his car. He really was a nice man. A little silly — not at all like Maria imagined her own father would be — but nice. How he was the father of two such different children Maria would never understand. But then, she supposed she and Rafi didn't exactly have that much in common, either.

Maria took the banana pudding to the fridge and found her mother at the kitchen table, staring off into space again.

"You okay?" Maria asked.

"What? Oh, yeah," her mom replied. "Just thinking."

"Mrs. McCormick sent over another banana pudding."

"But we haven't even touched the last one."

Maria held up her hands as if to say, *What did you want me to do? Send it back?*

"So Rob is here?"

"Yeah, he went back to Rafi's room."

"Good," Mom said. "I'm glad Rafi is able to do some laughing tonight."

"What does that mean?"

"Oh, nothing. I just worry about you kids sometimes. One death is a lot, but two? I don't want you and your brother growing up thinking life is this big, sad thing."

"I don't think that," Maria said. "I laugh all the time."

"Do you?" Mom said, looking at Maria earnestly.

Maria laughed. "Yes, Mom. See?" She tugged at the edge of her shirt. "Derek makes me laugh," she said quietly.

"That's true. Derek is a good egg."

"He seemed a little weird this morning."

"At the funeral?"

Maria nodded.

"Well, he was very close to your grandmother, too, you know. Grief affects us all differently."

"Yeah," Maria said. She could hear the steady *thwack thwack* of two wooden swords from the direction of Rafi's room.

Mom drifted back to thinking whatever she was thinking, and Maria left her to it.

She slipped back into her room and pulled down one of her favorite books, *Agatha at Sea*, about a royal kitchen maid who finds a sword in the castle moat and becomes a pirate. Rereading her favorite books always made her feel happy and safe, because she already knew what would happen in the end. She wished that real life could work that way — that she could see the future, and that the future she saw would be always happy.

Tonight, Maria was having a hard time focusing on reading. Her eyes kept drifting over to her nightstand, where the spider ring was hiding in its box. Finally, she set her book down in defeat, promising herself that she'd just look at the ring for a second and then put it away.

She took out the ring and slipped it on her finger. It was no longer warm, which was a small relief. Hopefully that meant it hadn't tried to do any magic without her.

Maria made her breath as quiet as possible. She cupped her hands behind her ears, supposing that maybe she'd be able to hear the spiders the way she'd started to last night. But Maria heard nothing. Even the dueling sounds from her brother's room had stopped.

Maria was shocked to discover that she knew why. Rafi and Rob were on their way to her room.

She followed the faint tremors of their footsteps as they tiptoed down the hallway and up to her door. It wasn't that she could *see* them, exactly, or that she'd had a premonition of something that would happen soon — it was that she could *feel* the vibrations, actually, physically, as if the house were her web and Rob and Rafi had stumbled into it.

She stared at her door a full second before Rafi pushed it open. Instantly, her brother took a step backward and gasped.

"What are you doing?" he said, his voice cracking. Rob stood beside and a little behind him. Both boys looked terrified.

"What do you mean?" Maria asked, smoothing out the blanket on the bed next to her, mostly so she could hide her hand under her pillow and slip off the ring.

"You were staring at something, and your eyes . . ."

"My eyes what? What are you talking about, Rafi?"

"It looked like your eyes were totally black," Rob said. Rafi seemed to have gone mute.

"Very funny," Maria said. She didn't think the boys were kidding, but she hoped if she could convince them she did, they would drop the subject.

After a long pause, Rob smiled, and Rafi said, "Don't do that again, whatever it was. It was *creepy*."

Maria laughed, doing her best impression of someone who wasn't afraid. "Whatever you say."

"Hey, look at that," Rob said, pointing at something over Maria's shoulder. She followed his finger and saw, in the far corner of her ceiling, the biggest spiderweb she had ever seen. She didn't know how she'd missed it earlier.

"Man, Maria, Mom's going to be mad when she sees you didn't clean your room," Rafi chided.

"I did too clean my room," Maria said. "And if you tell her about this, I'll tell her you snuck in my room and tried to scare me."

Rafi stuck out his tongue at her.

"It's a good thing my sister's not here to see this," Rob said. "She *hates* spiders. What's that thing called when you're afraid of them?"

"Arachnophobia?" Maria said.

"Yeah, that's it. Claire is totally that."

Maria felt something click in the back of her brain. An idea was forming there, and she was a little ashamed of it, but she told herself it was more of a dream than a plan. At least, for now.

"Are you going to her party tomorrow?" Maria asked Rob.

"Ew, no," he said. "I heard Claire tell one of her friends that she was hoping they'd play truth or dare. I don't want to be anywhere near that party."

Maria started to ask something else, but Rafi seemed annoyed that his friend and his sister were having a conversation without him, so he grabbed Rob by the arm and said, "Come on, let's go back to my room." Just like that, they left Maria alone.

She jumped up and looked in her mirror. Her eyes weren't black, except in the middle where they were always black. They were brown and normal. She'd really been scared for a second there.

She decided she wouldn't grab the broom and take down the spiderweb on the ceiling. As strange as it was, she had to believe the spiders were her friends. And if she was going to pull off her idea, which was seeming less and less like a dream and more and more like a full-fledged plan, she was going to need her new friends' help.

She brushed her teeth quickly and got ready for bed. She pulled out the ring from under her pillow and slipped it back on, climbing under her covers.

She turned out the light and closed her eyes. In the darkness, she began to imagine another beautiful dress. This one wasn't for a funeral, though. The dress in her head was a party dress.

CHAPTER 9

As Maria made her way to English class the next day, she was playing a little game in her head. The game was like one of those books where the story changes based on the choices you make — if you open the locked chest, turn to page fifty-three. On page fifty-three, a snake jumps out and bites you. The end.

The choices that were playing in Maria's head had to do with whether or not Claire was nice to her today. If Claire was nice to her, Maria would forget her whole plan. But if Claire was mean . . .

Maria smoothed out the folds in her new dress. She'd decided that it was too pretty not to wear to school, even though that meant wearing a jacket to cover her arms, and getting the knee-length skirt a little wrinkled on the bus.

She reached her classroom. She walked through the door.

She saw Claire's face.

For the tiniest fraction of a second, Claire's eyes went soft and her mouth turned down, registering sympathy for Maria's loss. But then, like one of those movies they'd watched in science that shows a flower dying in fast-forward, Claire's face twisted into jealousy before decomposing into a quiet rage.

Maria could guess why Claire was jealous. She got to the front of her row and did a confident twirl, letting the hem of her dress spiral out like a movie star's. Her classmates all locked their eyes on her, enthralled. It was the first time they'd seen her since Grandma Esme had died.

But for the moment, the only reaction that really mattered was Claire's, and Claire's face looked like the snake from page fifty-three, ready to strike.

"Nice dress," she sneered, although she was unable to hide all the envy from her voice. "Where'd you get it, the dollar store?"

"It's from Europe, actually," Maria said, sitting down.

Claire choked on a laugh, then lapsed into silence for a full ten seconds. She turned to Mark and Tina. "Don't forget, my party's at six thirty," she said. "All the *cool* people will be there."

Mark and Tina smiled, but they looked a little nervous, too. They — and the rest of the class — could feel that something had changed in Maria. Something that went deeper than just a strange and expensive new outfit. Maria had *power*. Claire's insults practically bounced off her.

Maria faced the front of the class with a smile.

Let them wonder, she thought. *Let them feel like outcasts for a change.*

"So I've decided we should go to Claire's party," Maria said at lunch. It was true, she had decided this, but at the moment she was trying mainly to get Derek's attention. He'd been staring at his food, hardly saying a word. He looked like Rafi had once when he'd gotten food poisoning.

"I thought we weren't invited," Derek said, almost bored.

"Well, *I* wasn't. I mean, I'm still not. I've decided I want to *crash* Claire's party."

"Why would you want to do that?" Derek held the same silver dollar from earlier in the week. He gripped it in his right hand like he was afraid he might drop it.

"Is everything okay?" Maria asked, though she felt weird saying it. Usually in their friendship, he was the one who made sure she was okay.

"Yeah, everything's fine. I just don't understand why you'd want to go to a party where you're not wanted."

He didn't sound like Derek at all.

"I heard about a special surprise that was happening, and I thought it might be fun to see."

"Heard where?"

"Um, from Claire? In English? Or maybe Rob told me. I can't remember."

Clearly, Derek didn't believe her. "Does this 'surprise' have anything to do with your magic ring?" he said. She did her best to keep her face totally blank.

"No," she lied. "Rob spent the night with Rafi last

night, and he said this thing about . . . Never mind. Forget I said anything."

"Are you still going to bring it by my dad's shop?" Derek said, ignoring her outburst. "Grandma Esme's ring?"

"If I do, will you start acting normal?" Maria snapped.

Derek seemed like he was about to snap right back, but then thought better of it.

"Yes," he said. "I mean, sorry. It's been weird not having you at school this week. I've been worrying about you and that ring. And now you show up in this fancy dress, saying you want to go to Claire McCormick's birthday party? It just doesn't seem like you."

If Maria had been surprised before, this sudden role reversal really caught her off guard.

"Don't worry about me," she said. "I'm still the same Maria. And if that stops being true, you'll be the first to know."

Derek nodded. He spun the silver dollar on the table, and he and Maria watched it until it finally wobbled and fell on its side, heads up.

"I'll have my mom bring me by the shop after dinner," Maria said.

"And then, if you really still want to, we can go crash Claire's party."

"Really?"

"Really. I wouldn't want to miss this special surprise."

Maria smiled. "If it's half as good as Rob said, you'll never forget it."

Maria had no problem convincing her mom to take her to the shop, in yet another dress she claimed to have gotten from Grandma Esme. After what her mother had said last night about wanting them all to enjoy life, Maria probably could have asked for the car keys and driven herself.

With a quick call to Derek's parents to let them know they were on the way, Maria and her mother hopped in the car and drove to the historic downtown district. Maria loved this part of town, over by the railroad tracks. You could still see the original brick roads peeking out where there were holes in the asphalt, and the old-timey streetlamps looked as if they could be powered by gas. Maria liked to picture the people who would have shopped here when it was the only place to go, before there were cars and outlet malls.

"Derek's dad said he'd bring you home when you're ready," Mom said. "Have fun."

Maria walked up to the front door of the shop, sandwiched in between two large display windows. There were a few new items since the last time Maria had been here. An eerie porcelain doll sat on a rocking horse with chipped paint. Maria couldn't imagine anyone in this town buying either item, but you never knew. Sometimes the most ordinary people liked the strangest things.

It was five o'clock now, which meant the shop would be open for another hour. Derek's family usually hung around after closing on Friday nights, though, checking inventory and setting up displays for the weekend shoppers. Saturday was a busy day for the historic district.

The old cowbell above the door clunked as Maria entered.

"Well, look who it is, dressed all nice to see us," Mr. Overton called from behind the counter. He stepped out to meet her by the front tables. "I'm so glad you're here. We just got in a necklace this morning that made me think of you." He reached out his hand as if to pat her on the shoulder, but then, so fast she could hardly see it, he'd clasped the necklace around her neck. It was a string of black and purple rocks with little silver beads in between.

"Wow," Maria said, "it's so pretty. But there's no way I could afford this, even with the family discount."

"Are you kidding?" Derek's dad said. "This beautiful necklace was clearly made special to go with this beautiful dress. Let's call it a gift."

It was true, the match was perfect.

"Oh, Mr. Overton, my mom would never let me accept this."

"Please," he said, waving his hand like it was nothing. "Besides, those look like gemstones, but they're really just colored rocks. I couldn't sell it for more than twenty dollars."

"All right, then," Maria said, laughing. "Thank you." Fake rocks or not, it was still the third-nicest gift anyone had ever given her.

"Derek's downstairs," Mr. Overton said, nodding to the door in the back that led to the basement. "And do me a favor when you see him? Tell him to lighten up."

So Maria wasn't the only one who'd noticed Derek's recent mood swings. That made her feel a little bit better, and a whole lot worse.

"Will do," she said, making her way through the maze of display tables.

She descended the steps to the cavernous basement. All the buildings in the historic district had these carved-out, cave-like spaces beneath them. They were never open to the public because the sandy Florida soil made them a little unstable. Nowadays, it was rare to find a basement in any Florida building at all.

The Overtons used their basement for the antiques they were still polishing, painting, or otherwise restoring. Maria always thought it looked like a dragon's horde down here. The old mirrors scattered around only added to the effect, multiplying the space and the treasure infinitely.

"Derek? Are you down here?" Maria called out at the bottom of the stairs.

"Maria!" Derek said, appearing from behind a bookcase with the sound of crashing objects trailing in his wake. He held an old clock in one hand and a wrench in the other, and he was scratching at his neck as if he'd just hit it on something. "What are you doing here so early? I thought you weren't coming over until after dinner."

"Mom had such a busy day she forgot to eat lunch, so we ate an early dinner. We called fifteen minutes ago to say we were on the way."

"My dad didn't tell me."

"Oh. Well, sorry. Do you want me to go?" She said it jokingly, but Derek hurt her feelings by actually seeming to consider. "Your dad says you should lighten up, by the way."

Derek frowned. Then he asked, "Did you bring Grandma Esme's ring?"

"It's my ring now, and yes, I did. Just like I promised. Any moment now, you're going to stop acting weird, just like *you* promised."

Derek looked around skittishly.

"You're right," he said, scratching his neck again. "It's just, I thought you were coming later."

"Well, Claire's party starts in less than an hour, so . . ."

They stood there staring at each other, as if they were having an argument instead of a conversation between friends. For the life of her, Maria couldn't figure out what the argument was.

"So did you want to show my ring to your dad? See if he can tell us anything?"

"No, that's okay," Derek said. "Aunt Luellen is the one with all the jewelry knowledge, and she's out right now."

"Why would Aunt Luellen know anything about jewelry?"

"She's an appraiser. That's what she does in New York, and all over the world. She works for one of those big auction houses, telling them how much to sell things for. Stuff that's a lot more valuable than anything around here."

"I like the stuff here," Maria said, her hand going to the rock necklace at her neck. Now she knew something was really wrong with her best friend. The Derek she knew would never insult his family's shop. "Well, is your aunt getting back before Claire's party?"

"I don't know," Derek said. "She left to go see her friend again. She didn't say when she was coming back."

"Okay, then," Maria said, feeling increasingly exasperated. She nodded to the wrench in Derek's hand. "What are you working on?"

"This? It's nothing. Just fixing up an old clock. Come on, do you want to head upstairs and walk around outside? I feel like I've been in this basement forever."

Maria couldn't agree more. She followed Derek around the piles of antiques back toward the stairs, but jerked his arm suddenly when she saw a spiderweb in their path.

"Whoa, what gives?" he said, rubbing his arm.

"You almost walked right into that web."

"Oh, wow. I didn't even see it."

He leaned in to take a closer look at the web just as Maria located the spider that had made it. The spider was looking right at her, but she could still see its body, and its bloodred hourglass.

"Derek, don't!" she exclaimed. "That's a black widow spider. Their bites are poisonous."

Derek jumped away.

"Jeez. Thanks, M. Now I *really* think it's time to go."

He grabbed her hand and started to lead her around the web. It was strange, she thought, that he didn't at least want to cut the thing down.

"Derek, wait."

"Seriously? You want to stay down here with a poisonous spider?"

"It's just . . . if a black widow bites you, my mom says you can go thirty whole minutes before you feel it. I noticed you scratching your neck earlier. Do you think the spider could have already bitten you?"

"What? No way. I'm fine, Maria. But I might not be if we stay down here a second longer."

"Do you want me to take a look at your neck?"

"I said I'm *fine*."

"All right, all right," Maria said. She didn't want to be down here another moment, either, with the black widow spider she could swear had been watching her. She let Derek pull her up the stairs that led back to the shop. She waved helplessly to Mr. Overton as Derek gave him a very gruff good-bye, mumbling that they were going to grab root beer floats at the old-fashioned pharmacy down the block.

Outside, the sun was just beginning to set, the pinks and reds reaching out to them like fire filtered through a gemstone. Maria remembered what her mom had said about old people who got more confused as the sun went down. Could it happen to young people, too? Would Derek be warning her about lurking enemies next?

And if being confused was the first sign of something worse, would Maria be able to save him, the way she hadn't been able to save Grandma Esme?

CHAPTER 10

Distance from the shop seemed to do Derek good. Root beer floats seemed to do him even better. By the time his float was a creamy soda at the bottom of a tall glass, Derek was almost back to his chipper self.

"So remind me what the plan is for Claire's party?" he said, raising his voice in a question at the end. "We're just going to walk up and act like we're totally welcome there? Won't that be really unpleasant for you?"

"It *would* be unpleasant, which is why we're not going to do that. We're going to sneak around the entrance by the lake and hide behind Claire's pool house until the 'surprise' happens."

Derek's eyes widened. He coughed on the last sip of root beer float.

"You're joking."

"What?" Maria said. "I've been over there with Rafi before. I know my way around. And we won't have to be there for very long."

"Oh, well, that makes the thought of trespassing on Claire's property so much better."

"Come on, Derek. Please? You know you want to see Claire get what she deserves."

"You still haven't told me what that is, exactly."

"I told you, it's a surprise."

"If you want me to come with you, you at least have to give me a hint."

"Fine," Maria said, sipping the last of her own float. She tried to think of the best way to put this. "Let's just say you and I won't be the only unexpected guests at the party."

Maria hadn't been lying when she'd said she'd been here before, to the narrow gravel driveway that led around the McCormicks' lake. But that had been in the daytime, in her mother's jeep, dropping Rafi off. She hadn't been trying to walk on uneven rocks in a fancy dress that time, shivering in the cold. She also hadn't paid any attention to the forks in the path.

"Are you sure it was supposed to be a left back there?" Derek whispered. Maria didn't have the heart to tell him they had a while yet before he needed to be quiet.

"Pretty sure."

"Are we almost there?"

"Yup, almost," she replied, deciding to sound more confident than she felt.

"I don't think my dad believed me when I said we were walking back home. Do you?"

"I thought he did," Maria said. "Why else would he have let us leave on our own?"

"Because he feels sorry for you."

"Oh." The syllable fell out of her mouth like a heavy, dead thing.

"No, I mean, because of . . . this week."

"I know what you meant," she said. Her voice was clipped.

"Well, either way, as long as we make it back in an

hour, we should be good. Is the surprise supposed to happen before then?"

"I think so. And if not, I'm sure that could be arranged."

"Okay. I've got my phone just in case we run late."

"We might need to use it as a flashlight soon."

It was a few minutes past six thirty, and the last hints of sunlight had vanished into the February air. When she thought Derek wasn't looking, Maria slipped the ring out of her clutch purse and slid it onto her finger. *If you're listening,* she thought, *please show us the way before we get lost.*

The familiar warmth of the ring was welcome in the chill, and Maria sensed the spiders before she saw them. It was as if the blades of grass at her feet weren't tiny but massive, quaking with the vibrations stirred by the creatures' approach. Her eyes went right to them — two, then a few, then a multitude of spiders, weaving and scuttling through the grass and the leaves.

She tried to follow them without being too obvious. She didn't want Derek to know the full extent of the ring's powers, for reasons she couldn't fully explain. She used to feel like she could trust him with anything.

When they came to the next fork, Maria eyed the line of shiny silver spiders at her feet and said to Derek, "It's a right here. I'm positive this time."

Sure enough, after they cleared one final bend around a corner of trees, they could see the lights of the pool house and the house beyond it. The spiders veered off into the woods beside them. They must have decided Maria didn't need them anymore, now that she could see where she was going. But when Maria peered into the trees, she could swear she saw a pair of eyes staring back at her, hovering in the shadows, beckoning for her to follow.

"Come on, Maria," Derek said, standing at her side. "What are you looking at?"

The eyes were gone, although Maria hadn't sensed any movement. Maybe she'd imagined them after all.

"Nothing, sorry."

Maria and Derek hurried up behind the pool house. Really, it was more like a pool*side* house, small only in relation to the McCormicks' mansion on the other side of the yard. There was even a little kitchen visible through the back window. Pressing her face against that window and peering through to the front, Maria could see the large mass of kids from school, crowded on a glass dance floor over the pool, just as Claire had promised. A few people danced, but mostly people stood around in clumps, like they were at a dance in the school gym. The blue glow from the pool and a string of lights overhead made everyone look like they were underwater. The effect was dazzling.

"I think we might be the only kids in our grade *not* at this party," Derek said.

For a frightening moment, Maria couldn't breathe. The sight of everyone she knew having such a good time without her struck her like a punch in the stomach when she wasn't ready. She had known in her head that Claire didn't like her, and it had been easy to say that she didn't care. But this felt like a real, physical pain — one she couldn't control with words. What had she done to deserve this? Nothing, that's what. Claire was a mean girl, end of story.

"You okay?" Derek asked.

"Sure," Maria said, breathing in, then out, the way Grandma Esme had taught her to do during yoga. "I'm getting more and more excited to see the surprise."

But when Maria scanned the crowd for Claire, she found her standing off to one side, not smiling or talking to anyone in particular. She actually looked a little nervous, as if after working so hard to plan the perfect party, Claire had no energy left to enjoy the party itself. The playlist she'd made echoed over four speakers surrounding the mass of guests. It looked like people were having a hard time hearing one another.

"Honestly, it doesn't seem all that fun," Derek said, echoing her thoughts. It was almost revenge enough to know that Claire's perfect party wasn't so perfect after all. But only almost. Because Maria had a feeling that come Monday, Claire would somehow remember that the party had been amazing — that Maria had missed out on the time of her life — and she would bully everyone else into remembering the same thing.

No, Maria needed to bring Claire off her fairy-princess pedestal, so that she'd never be able to bully her the same way again. She needed to do something that no one would be able to forget.

After at least ten minutes of watching the party unfold, during which Derek kept looking anxiously at the clock on his phone and asking Maria when the surprise was going to happen, Maria finally saw Claire's mom coming out of the house, carrying a birthday cake with thirteen candles lit on top.

The crowd parted to let Mrs. McCormick through, and after the music was brought to an abrupt stop, the whole party joined in on a loud rendition of "Happy Birthday to You." Maria could almost feel the force of their voices on her skin, and it made her want to hurry, to stop the singing. She clasped her hands together, twisting the spider ring around her finger. She spoke to the spiders in a frenzy, under her breath — asking, then begging, for them to come and help her.

Mrs. McCormick reached the table that held the rest of the food and set the cake down next to Claire. Smiling thinly, Claire moved her hair behind one ear and bent over the cake.

The party sang for Claire. Wishing her a happy birthday.

Then three things happened all at once:

The seventh-grade chorus hit the last *to you* like a

train crash, a cacophony of notes and at least three animal noises from the sillier boys in their school.

Claire took a deep breath and prepared to blow out her candles.

And a brown mass of spiders skittered quickly up the table onto the cake and Claire's dress.

Chaos erupted. Claire screamed like Maria had never heard anyone scream before. Other people screamed, too, some because they were in the front and could see what was going on, the rest because they couldn't see at all and were afraid of what must be happening just out of sight.

Through all the shouting, Maria could hear the steady undercurrent of another sound, distinct and distinctly not human. It was the spiders talking. They sounded eager, proud.

"No way," Derek said, no longer bothering to be quiet. "Maria, how did you know — oh my gosh, Maria!"

Derek grabbed her by the shoulders and shook. The force of his grip registered as if from a dream. She blinked and tried to focus on him, realizing that her vision had gone blurry.

"Maria, your eyes were *black*," Derek said. He sounded more angry than scared.

"That's crazy," Maria said, but she was hardly paying attention to him. She walked around to the side of the pool house — she couldn't see well enough through the windows.

The screaming had stopped. Claire was lying faceup on the glass floor, and for a second, Maria's heart stopped. *She couldn't be . . .*

But no. Maria distinctly heard Mark Spitzer say the word "fainted," and Mrs. McCormick only looked mildly worried as she shook Claire's shoulders. Maybe this had even happened before, some other time when Claire had seen a spider. At least, that's what Maria was telling herself now, so she wouldn't feel so panicked.

"*You* did that," Derek said. "Claire's brother wasn't even outside."

Maria's attention snapped back to her friend, and she realized that he wasn't just angry — he was furious.

"What are you talking about?" Maria said. "I didn't have anything to do with it." Her voice was so confident in this deception, it made her a little queasy.

"It's the ring. Somehow you used that ring and you made that happen. Your eyes were totally black and you were — you were whispering. *Talking* to them."

"Come on, Derek. You don't really believe that."

"You're right," he said icily. "I can't *believe* you just dragged me all the way here so I could watch you ruin someone's party. And I can't *believe* that now you're trying to lie to me about it."

Maria felt tears collecting at the corners of her eyes. Derek had never talked to her this way, and it made all the bad things that had happened in the past week even worse. Or maybe it was just that all the hurt of the week hadn't fully caught up to her yet, but the shock of her best friend yelling at her made the reality impossible to ignore.

"No, Derek, listen —" she said, but he'd already turned around.

"Find your own way home," he said, stomping away. "Maybe your spiders will help you."

The spiders are your friends. Do not abuse their friendship.

Tonight, the spiders weren't the only ones whose friendship Maria had abused. She hadn't meant to let things get this far. Or, no, she *had* meant to — she'd just wanted a happier outcome.

Go away, she thought, seeing that a number of the spiders, *her* spiders, still lingered around Claire and the cake. *Now.*

She waited behind the pool house long enough to see that they obeyed her, and to see that Claire was waking up. Instantly, people crowded around her to ask if she was okay. Maria couldn't believe it: Even her humiliation was a cause for sympathy, another reason to worship her. If Maria had passed out at her own birthday party, people would be laughing behind her back — and to her face — for weeks.

Before anyone could see her, Maria hurried back down the gravel path through the woods. She didn't need the spiders to tell her where to go, but they appeared to lead the way anyway, scurrying in and out of her feet as she ran. She made sure not to step on any of them, even though it would have been so easy to. They were what Maria deserved. They were her only friends now.

Maria was so distracted staring at her feet, she didn't

notice the man in the black silk suit until she ran right into him.

She landed on her back. Quickly, she scrambled backward on the palms of her hands and tried to get a good look at the man in front of her.

With trembling lips and a face like a frightened rabbit's, he seemed to be even more surprised than she was.

Maria realized that she had seen this man before, at her grandmother's funeral. He'd been the one who'd disappeared in a cloud of shadow. There in one blink, gone the next.

He did it again now — *poof,* like magic — and the shock was so great it left Maria stunned. She had no idea how this man kept vanishing, but she was starting to have a pretty good idea of who he might be.

Getting to her feet, she brushed herself off. Her mom would be worried when Maria got back so late, but without a phone, she didn't really have a choice.

She put one foot in front of the other, and began the long walk home.

The spiders watched her as she went.

PART THREE

THE BLACK WIDOW

We are the spiders of the Order of Anansi.

We dwell in the dark places where dreams are made.

We follow the power and go where it goes

And watch our rewards come to us in the end.

CHAPTER 11

As long as the walk was, Maria would have done it all over again, right now, with her eyes closed, if it meant she didn't have to open the front door. But her legs ached and her eyes stung. If she wanted to get to her bedroom, she had to pass through the living room first. Maria took a deep breath and opened the door.

"Where in the world have you been, young lady?" her mother shouted, jumping up from the couch as if she'd been shot out of a cannon. She was fully dressed, even down to her hiking boots. Normally she'd be in sweatpants and a T-shirt by now.

"I had to walk all the way home from Claire's party. Maybe if I had a cell phone —"

"Oh, no, you are not blaming this on me. You were supposed to be at the store, and then you were supposed to come home. Derek's dad called me in a fit at seven because you two were supposed to have walked straight to their house. And *then*, he called me to say that Derek showed up with *no idea* where you were."

"That's because he left me," Maria said quietly.

"Left you where?"

"I told you, at Claire's party."

"Don't you lie to me, Maria! I know for a fact you were not at Claire's party. I had to go pick up your brother from her house after there was some kind of accident. He's back in his room now, and if you'd like to bring him out here and ask him whether you and Derek were at that party, be my guest."

"What, so you and Rafi can gang up on me, like always?" Maria said, her voice rising in a shrill crescendo. She felt ridiculous now in her black party dress, torn and dirty from her trek through the woods. It suddenly seemed like she was playing pretend, wearing the costume of an older girl from one of her stories. Right at this moment, she felt like she was eight years old.

"This has nothing to do with your brother," her mother said. "This has to do with you not being where you were supposed to be and not telling anyone where you were."

"You have no idea where Rafi is half the time! 'He's just over at Rob's house,' or 'Oh, he's *outside*, playing in the park,' which could mean anywhere. You're just mad at me because you think I'm weird, just like you thought Grandma Esme was weird. You think if I'm gone, I must be up to something bad."

Her mother sighed and slumped back down onto the couch. She rubbed her temples like Maria was giving her a headache. Finally, in a voice that was quiet but no less severe, she said, "Go to your room. You are grounded until I say otherwise."

"Good!" Maria shouted, now trying to sound unhinged on purpose. "I *love* being grounded!"

She stormed down the hallway, stopping when she found Rafi peeking his head out of his room. He looked scared.

"Where were you?" he asked.

"What do you care?" Maria snapped. She threw open her door and slammed it behind her. She paced back and forth in front of her bed, which usually calmed her down but now only worked her into more of a rage. She came to a halt in front of her mirror and glared at her reflection. She cut quite a frightening figure in her ragged black dress. There was a smudge on her face that looked like ash.

She wasn't playing dress-up. She really was the shadow queen, evil powers and all. And shadow queens didn't let mothers or brothers tell them what to do. What did Mom and Rafi know about being an outcast? What did they know about being abandoned by their friends?

Maria's thoughts continued down this spiral until her exhaustion finally caught up with her. She lay down on top of her comforter and fell into a sleep riddled with nightmares. Over her head, the spiders kept spinning, adding rows and layers to their web, unnoticed.

The whispers in her head finally woke Maria up, rising and rattling over one another like distant rain. She'd gone to sleep wearing the ring again. The correlation seemed obvious. If she took off the ring now, she would stop hearing the spider voices.

She didn't take off the ring.

The whispers were growing steadily louder. The closer Maria listened, the more she could make out individual voices from the cluster. None of them were speaking in words, exactly, or at least no words Maria knew. But their meaning was clear. They wanted Maria to follow them.

Stepping down from her bed, Maria found an unbroken line of them, crawling up and down the wall, in and out of the bedroom, so that they looked like a stream with currents flowing in both directions. It didn't matter that it was after midnight and completely dark; Maria could see the spiders as if they carried their own kind of light.

She got dressed quickly, then tiptoed down the hallway and into the kitchen. The spiders had found a crack in the wall by the sliding glass door that led into the backyard and the park beyond.

So that's how they've been getting into the house.

Quietly, carefully, Maria slid open the door and followed the spiders outside.

She reached the imaginary line where her yard ended and Falling Waters began. When her mom had forced her to play outside as a little girl, she used to pretend that this was the boundary between the good kingdom and the evil kingdom. Tonight, she wasn't half as afraid as she used to be. It was like she was walking under a spell — a spell that made her brave. Whether it was a good spell or a bad spell didn't seem important.

In no time, Maria was crossing the gravel path near the stream that fed the waterfall. Her feet crunched on leaves and palm fronds as she stepped off the main path and into the dense woods. The ground grew damp, and the spiders led her downstream to where the water was faster and more treacherous. Maria hardly noticed that her black flats were getting ruined. She was too focused on following the spiders to the very lip of the waterfall, where she found a progression of worn, smooth stones she'd never noticed before. Taken together, they almost looked like a staircase, leading down the rock face behind the waterfall and into the sinkhole far below.

The spiders showed her the way.

The rock steps were slick and uneven, but Maria took them confidently, one at a time. She followed the stairs down until the waterfall rushed over her head, then blocked the outside world altogether. When she reached the last stair, she lifted her eyes from her feet, and there, cut into the rock face, was a hole that looked like the mouth of a cave. Even her mom probably didn't know about this.

Maria followed the spiders deeper into the hole, her eyes taking in the dark details of the cave without a problem. Faded graffiti filled the walls, with letters and hearts spelling out a history of brave or reckless people who had discovered the cave before her. Tiny animal bones littered the ground, all of them completely covered in spiderwebs. The voices in Maria's head reached out in hunger.

Finally, Maria could walk no farther. The cave had narrowed into a dead end, where she found a collection of boxes and debris. None of it was covered in the dust and cobwebs that smothered everything else, and there was a plate of half-eaten meat sitting atop one of the boxes. If it had been here awhile, it would have already decayed.

All of this junk stirred a feeling in Maria, a feeling that crystallized into a memory. It was like she was back in Grandma Esme's living room, and she just needed to figure out the pattern to the chaos. There were even books and papers scattered about. Maria had half a mind to check for secret compartments.

The spiders began to gather around her. At first, she thought they were going for the meat. But no, they were forming a circle around one of the books — one already in the center of a crate, set apart.

The book was bound in leather and looked quite old. Picking it up, Maria saw that the cover was adorned with little beads of glass arranged in a symbol. Many of the beads had fallen off over the years, and some of their edges were rough to begin with, but if Maria squinted hard enough, she could make out the shape of a spider inside of a circle. She might have guessed.

The pages inside were yellowed with age. Corners and edges were ragged and torn, and some of the pages had been ripped out completely. Every page was filled with scribbles, sketches, and diagrams. There were detailed drawings of animal anatomy next to arcane weapons and mysterious plants. Maria could tell that the handwriting surrounding these drawings belonged not to one person, but to a countless many.

Some of the writing was in English, and some of it wasn't. Some of it looked neat and deliberate, while some of it looked hurried, even desperate. Either the many authors of this book had all worked on it together, or it had passed from one person down to the next through the years.

Maria came to a drawing near the back of the book that she recognized immediately. The voices in her head became a frantic buzz. There, in black ink, was her spider ring.

There were seven other spider rings drawn on these two pages, and each of them looked just a little bit different. One of the rings bore a spider whose legs and sternum were drawn in outline, and under that ring was written, *The Mirror*. Another ring had a spider that was shaded in around its four front legs. Under that ring was the label, *The Orb*.

The spider on Maria's ring had what looked like two lima beans on its back. She never would have described it that way before, but now that she saw the drawing, it was impossible to miss.

Maria's ring was labeled *The Brown Recluse*. The voices in her head said that this was right.

There were more interesting things about Maria's ring. For one, hers was the only spider that had six eyes instead of eight. For another, it was the only ring for which there were *two* drawings. One showed the ring exactly as it looked on her finger. The other showed the ring with the spider flipped open, revealing the secret container Maria had discovered. There was even a little arrow pointing to it. Next to the arrow, a long list of words had been written and crossed out, with different-colored inks suggesting that whenever a person wrote a word down, that person crossed out the one before it. The words included *hemlock*, *cyanide*, *arsenic*, and *nightshade*.

Maria gulped. They were all types of poison.

She turned the page, hoping for something more pleasant, but at that exact moment, what sounded like a falling rock echoed from the cave entrance. Maria had seen enough.

Against the will of the voices, she closed the book and yanked her hands from the cover. The book hit the crate on its spine, and Maria hurried to catch it before it toppled and crushed a cluster of spiders scrambling to get out of the way. That's when Maria realized — some of these spiders were brown recluses, with lima-bean backs and six minuscule eyes, but more, many more, of these spiders were *not*. Most of these spiders had the bulbous silver bodies of the mirror spider.

. . . Arturo would do the most unbelievable things with just a handkerchief and a mirror . . .

Oh, no —

Maria turned to rush out of the cave, already telling herself that when she got home and went to sleep, she would wake up and realize this had all been a terrible dream.

But she didn't make it out of the cave.

She'd taken all of two steps when a black shadow appeared and blocked her way.

The shadow flickered and swirled into the shape of a man — a man in a black silk suit who wore a spider ring of his own.

"They told me you'd be here," the man said coldly. He didn't look scared like he had in the woods. He looked like he was in total control.

There was no mistaking it. Maria had been caught.

CHAPTER 12

Maria took a step back, the heel of her foot catching the corner of one of the boxes.

"The Amazing Arturo," she said, unable to mask her wonder. He was unmistakably the man from the poster. It looked like he'd hardly aged since then; his slicked-back hair and severe eyebrows gave him the look of a black-and-white-film star. But unlike the dashing magician from the poster, the man standing before her wasn't smiling. The man before her had sharp, cruel eyes.

"I th-thought you were dead," Maria stammered.

"If it was up to me, you would still think that," he said.

"Are you going to kill me now? The way I bet you killed Grandma Esme?" She wasn't sure where this sudden boldness came from. She should probably be pleading for her life instead of giving him ideas about ending it. But the thought that this man had double-crossed Grandma Esme, had *killed* her over some *stupid* ring with *stupid* powers, made her so angry she didn't have any energy left to second-guess herself.

"What?" the man said, his frown giving way to surprise. "You think *I* killed Esmerelda? You don't know what you're talking about."

"I know that these rings help people do things they later regret. I know these rings can get in the way of friends."

Arturo sighed. "Well, you're right, there." He slumped down onto one of the boxes, planting his elbows on his knees and his chin in his hands. He reminded Maria of Rafi when Rafi was pouting. They had the same stormy eyes.

Maria inched her body to the left. Arturo looked just distracted enough that she might be able to slip past him and run. The rock steps would be tricky — Maria could already picture him grabbing her ankle as she tried to climb — but that seemed better than being killed in this forgotten cave.

"I'm not going to hurt you," Arturo said. Had he read her mind with his ring? She'd have to be more careful with her thoughts. "I wish you hadn't found my hideout," he continued, "but now that you have, and now that you think I . . . *murdered* Esmerelda — well, I suppose I had better explain a few things."

Maria wasn't sure. "How can I trust you?" she asked.

"You can't, obviously. But at least you've got the right questions. Keep your distrust. It will serve you well."

He looked so sad as he said this, Maria felt that she could . . . not *trust* him, exactly, but safely lean against this cave wall and hear him out. The second he tried to get up from that box, though, she was out of here.

"So if you didn't kill Grandma Esme, what are you doing here in Florida?"

Arturo tilted his head to the side, as if he was listening to something Maria couldn't hear. Maybe he and his spiders spoke at a different frequency. He said, "How much of that book did you read?"

"Enough to know that this isn't the only spider ring."

"Very good. There are eight rings — one for each of the members in the Order of Anansi."

"The order of a what?"

"*Anansi*. The spider god, trickster god, god of all stories. Perhaps you have heard the tale of the time he rescued stories from the sky god, only you forgot his name. You would not be the first. His name is as slippery and treacherous as he is."

"And you're saying this . . . Anansi . . . is real?"

"In a sense. When you tell a story enough times, it has a way of coming true, whether it was true in the first place or not."

Maria could see that. She doubted she herself could have become the shadow queen if she hadn't first known the stories about what shadow queens were.

"In any event, whether or not Anansi himself is real, the Order of Anansi most certainly is. And, as you have seen yourself, their powerful rings are quite real, too."

Maria looked down at the ring on her finger. For so long it had been *Grandma Esme's ring*, "a gift from a friend." The idea that it was actually an ancient relic that had been passed down through the years, like the book, made her a little dizzy.

"So you're saying you and Grandma Esme were part of this Order, and I never knew it?"

Arturo glanced around the cave, as if there might be some prop or picture that would help him explain. "How much did your grandmother tell you about her past with me?"

"Well, she said that she used to be a lion tamer, and you were a magician. And she said that you two used to travel around Europe doing your performances. I even found a poster from one of the shows. That's how I knew who you were." She half expected him to congratulate her on this point, as if she'd made some brilliant deduction. He hardly nodded. "Anyway, that's all."

"So she never told you the story of how we met?"

"No," Maria said sheepishly, like she'd gotten the answer wrong on a test. She felt silly and even a little embarrassed. Her grandmother had led a fascinating life, and while Maria had certainly appreciated her stories, she had never bothered to ask her for more.

"Then that's where we'll start. You might want to sit down."

Maria still didn't trust Arturo completely. If anything, she was even warier now. She knew that telling a story was like spinning a spiderweb. A good storyteller could lure you in, and before you knew it, it was too late — you were trapped. Maria would listen to Arturo's story, but she wouldn't let herself get lost in it. She was lost in too many stories already.

"All right," Arturo said. "Many years ago, in the city of Cahul . . ."

ARTURO'S STORY

The sun had barely crested the hill on Strada Denoir when Arturo came bounding down the stairs and out the door to his bicycle.

The tiny house they shared with the Marandici family had such pitiful insulation, it hardly protected them all from the winter cold, let alone from the echo of footsteps and arguments. When one person in the house got up for the day, everyone did. Which meant that if Arturo had woken up just a few minutes later, or if he had taken longer to get ready, Nadia and Alec Marandici would have beaten him out here, and he and his bicycle would have been stuck for hours.

Arturo stuffed the brown paper package with the lamb shank in his basket, then placed the brown paper packages with the cotton shirt and the lace gloves on top. He'd learned the hard way what happened if he got the order wrong, when he'd pulled out the socks for Mrs. Saguna and found them covered in beef juice. His family had eaten poorly that week.

Today, two of his three deliveries were going to the same place. The Ionescus had been one of the first families willing to pay for their meat and their stitching to be delivered, and they were still some of Arturo's best customers. He liked riding his bicycle to their house because Mrs. Ionescu always gave him a piece of candy. The Ionescus *never* ate poorly.

Because he'd left his house so early, Arturo still had a few hours left before he and his packages would be welcome. He rode through town, where the rising sun on the stone pillars and archways always made him feel like he was somewhere else, somewhere magical. Somewhere where war hadn't planted its deep roots in the ground.

Once, when he was little, and Cahul was still a Russian city, Arturo had seen a parade of soldiers march down this very street. The display had been meant to inspire the city's citizens, but Arturo had been more afraid than moved. Today, the city's history of territorial disputes still peeked out everywhere in Cahul. There were even soldiers from the Great War in the city hospital, some of them on the mend, some of them only biding their time.

As he rode by the hospital now, Arturo saw a girl about his own age leaning out of the window. She was emptying a bedpan, but the sight of Arturo on his bicycle left her slack-jawed and gaping. Arturo was used to that. Bicycles were rare in Cahul, especially among kids. He was only allowed to have one because his parents couldn't make the deliveries themselves.

Not wanting the lamb to spoil, Arturo decided it was time to stop dawdling. As always, the Ionescus' sprawling brick house took his breath away. Arturo left his bicycle on the sidewalk and went to knock on their door.

"Arturo, good morning," said Mrs. Ionescu. "Come in. Would you like a candy?"

"Yes, please," Arturo said, and she smiled. It was always easier to show good manners when he wasn't around his own family. He followed Mrs. Ionescu inside with a brown paper package in each hand.

"Dimitri is just getting up, but I'm sure he would be happy to see you as well. He was just asking me yesterday when you were coming again . . ."

When Arturo left the house nearly a half hour later, already wondering when he would get to come back, he saw right away that his bicycle was gone. How could he have been so stupid! Of *course* someone had taken it. Wouldn't he have done the same thing?

After he'd searched the whole block, Arturo finally gave up. He'd just have to make the deliveries on foot. Either that, or his family would starve.

About a week or so later, after Arturo had endured punishment from his father, two calloused feet from his deliveries, and one insufferable day of gloating from Alec and Nadia, a girl appeared at their door. She had his bicycle in tow.

"I found it near my house," she said, looking Arturo right in the face. "I could tell from the shirt that it must belong to you." She handed him a brown paper package with a shirt tucked inside.

"You found me from one cotton shirt?" Arturo said.

"It's not many people who deliver cotton in butcher paper."

Arturo wrapped his fingers around his handlebars, recalling the wonderful feeling of power and speed. But the girl hadn't let go yet.

"Why do I feel like I've seen you before?" Arturo asked.

"Because you did see me. I didn't think you'd remember, though. I work at the hospital with my mom. She's a proper nurse. I just clean the rooms and keep people company."

"Well, thanks for bringing my bicycle back. You don't know how much I needed this."

"Yes," the girl said, picking at a hole in the sleeve of her threadbare dress, "I do."

That was the day Arturo and Esmerelda became friends. It was years before Esmerelda admitted she hadn't found the bicycle at all. In fact, she'd stolen it, and returned it only when she heard from Nadia Marandici that the Antonescu boy had lost his bicycle and been punished for it.

* * *

They rode their bicycles to the mineral springs for months, ignoring the swiftly changing tides of the world. It wasn't until Esmerelda's tire caught on a rock one day that they discovered the cave.

"Your knee is bleeding," Arturo said, running over to help her back to her feet.

"It's just a scratch," Esmerelda said, taking his hand.

Once again, they'd been going too fast. That's what happened when Arturo let Esmerelda get in front. Seventeen years old, and still she was no closer to acting like a young lady than she had been when they met. Now her front wheel was bent beyond function, and they were stranded on the far side of the lake just as raindrops were starting to fall. It would take them many hours to walk home.

"Let's take cover in there," Arturo said, pointing to an opening in the rock beside them. Ferns and grass grew almost completely over the entrance, as if no one had been in the cave for a long time.

"How far back do you think it goes?" Esmerelda asked, leading them in without waiting for his answer.

Fortunately, the cave wasn't very deep at all. They could still see by the light trickling in from outside when they reached the back. And what they saw there was surprising indeed. Uniforms, weapons, wooden chests of supplies — all of it buried under a thick layer of cobwebs. It looked like they'd found a military outpost.

"Do you think these are from this war, or the last one?" Esmerelda said, brushing away a web and picking up a sword that still looked sharp.

"Neither one," Arturo said, though he suspected she'd been joking. "I think this is all much older. Just look at this map." He angled the crumbling parchment in his hands so that she could see it over his shoulder. The map depicted the Ottoman Empire, a place Arturo only knew about from history class.

"How are we ever going to get it all back?"

"Back? You mean, you want to *take* this stuff? I guess once a thief, always a thief."

"How many times do I have to tell you I'm sorry about that?" Esmerelda asked. She didn't sound very sorry anymore.

"I just worry about what will happen when the owners of this stuff come looking for it. What if they're pirates? Or killers? That's how it would go in a story."

"Well, this isn't a story. And no one has been here in ages, clearly. Unless you count the spiders."

Arturo wasn't convinced.

"Fine. What if we each just take *one* thing?" she said.

"One thing?"

"Just one. I already know what I'm picking."

Esmerelda grabbed a necklace with a purple stone pendant and placed it over her head. The necklace looked stunning on her.

"All right, then. You win, as usual," Arturo said, laughing. "What about this?" He grabbed an old officer's coat from one of the chests. When he pushed his arms through the sleeves, he was amazed to discover that it was a perfect fit.

"You were *meant* to find it," Esmerelda said.

Arturo smiled. The past few months had been so full of uncertainty, it was wonderful for something to feel like it made sense.

"Now come on," she said. "The rain has stopped, and I can ride back on your handlebars. We'll come back here later with a tool to fix my bicycle."

They left the cave then, giddy with their discoveries. But they would never see this cave, or Esmerelda's bicycle, again.

A few nights later, in the quiet of his room, Arturo put on his coat once more, imagining that he really was a storied officer and not a boy about to become a pawn — either for the Germans or for the Russians, it hardly seemed to matter.

He felt a knot poking him in the ribs, and at first, he thought it must be a stray button. But when there was no button in sight, Arturo realized there must be something inside the lining of the coat. Knowing that his mother could always sew it back up, Arturo retrieved a knife from the kitchen and cut into the fabric. Inside, he discovered a hidden pocket made from a fine, white silk that seemed awfully extravagant for something not meant to be seen. He turned the pocket over.

Two rings fell into his hand.

They were rings unlike any Arturo had ever seen. In place of jewels, each ring had a large, lifelike spider. One had long, thin legs and a kind of plate armor on its back; the other had tiny legs but a large glass body.

Arturo couldn't imagine why these rings had been hidden away in the secret pocket of this coat. He finally decided it was so that he could discover them — that just like the coat itself, he had been *meant* to find them.

Arturo knew what these rings were for. It couldn't wait. He had to see Esmerelda.

"I just don't understand why we have to leave like this, in the middle of the night, without a word to our parents."

"Fine, we can leave them notes."

Esmerelda crossed her arms. Her eyes darted to her bedroom door, as if her parents might be on the other side listening in.

"You know what I mean," she said.

"I don't think you understand how serious this is, Esmerelda. In another week, I could be off fighting, and then it won't matter how much we love each other or whether we have our parents' blessing."

Esmerelda bit her lip and scowled. It was the face she often made when she was reading a book and came to a part she didn't like.

"This all sounds very dangerous, Arturo."

"That's exactly why I thought you'd be excited."

"It is sort of exciting, isn't it?" she said, cracking a smile. Then she seemed to remember where she was. "But how will we make any money? What will we do?"

"We could sell these rings," Arturo said.

Esmerelda looked down at the ring on her left hand. Arturo had taken his mother's ash-wood box — the one in which she stored needles in one end and thread in the other — and placed the ring that looked more like Esmerelda in it. In the other end, he'd written her a note, so that she could read, rather than hear, the question: *Will you marry me?*

"I don't want to sell the ring," she said finally. "I only just got it."

"Then we'll figure something else out. Esmerelda, you have to trust me."

Neither of them could imagine the web that had drawn them in from that night onward. A web as old as war and as deadly, too.

In accepting these rings, Arturo and Esmerelda had forever changed the course of their lives. They believed they were embarking upon a new story, when in fact they had been drawn into a story already long in place.

"For that is the blessing and the curse of youth, you must understand," Arturo told Maria now. "Believing that no one else has lived your story before, and no one else will live it again. But I have been where you are now, Maria. I used my powers without regard for the consequences, and I was found out, just as you have been."

"Found out by you?" Maria asked.

Arturo sadly shook his head. "I wish it were only by me. I am not your enemy. But the Black Widow — the Black Widow knows you have the ring. She killed Esmerelda . . . and now she is after you."

CHAPTER 13

She'd held off through his entire story, but now, at the end, Maria finally sat down.

"So you and Grandma Esme were married?" she said.

Arturo didn't respond. He spun his ring around his finger.

"I still don't understand. Who is the Black Widow? A person?"

"In most senses, but not all. The Black Widow is the most powerful and treacherous of all in the Order of Anansi. For years, she has been hunting down the other members of the Order and killing them for their rings."

"Why?"

"The rings all draw their power from the spiders, but they each have their own special qualities, as unique as their species. A person who has more than one ring increases her or his power exponentially. According to legend, a person who collects all eight rings will have power to rival that of Anansi himself."

"'Legend' meaning that book?" Maria said, nodding toward the leather tome.

"Well, yes, I suppose so. But that book contains the knowledge of many generations of the Order. I myself have annotated it with the things I have learned. In all that time, no single person has obtained all eight rings. As of right now, the Black Widow has six."

"You mean, the only two rings she doesn't have are yours and mine?"

Arturo nodded. Finally, Maria could see why he looked so sad.

"How do you know all this? I mean, I'm guessing you didn't write that book yourself."

"You guess correctly. Esmerelda and I didn't sell our rings, of course. We discovered their magic after joining the Rimbaud Brothers, and it was only a short matter of time before we had climbed the ranks from cleaning the elephants' slop to starring in the show, putting our powers on display as if they were cheap parlor tricks. When we were first confronted, it was not by the Black Widow, but by the Orb Weaver."

Maria remembered the drawing of the orb ring from the book. She tried to imagine the kind of person who might have worn it, but the problem was, the rings could belong to anyone. It's not like there was any meaningful connection between the nature of the rings and the nature of the people who found them. She had to believe that.

More importantly, whoever had worn the orb ring back then couldn't be the person still wearing it now. The Black Widow had the ring. Maria gulped.

Arturo continued his tale. "The Orb Weaver was a well-meaning gentleman named Adrian Eberly. Our troupe was in Sion for a week of performances, and this man, Mr. Eberly, had read about Esmerelda and me in the paper. He guessed right away what we were meddling with. I'll never forget it — he found us in our tent, claiming to be an admirer and wondering if he could speak to us privately. But no sooner had we welcomed him in and offered to hang his coat than he turned to us and said, sure as death, 'You have rings, don't you?'

"At first, we pretended to have no idea what he was talking about. But Mr. Eberly was no fool. He beckoned his orb weavers, one by one, and they came hurrying into the tent in an obedient line until they had filled every inch of the ground around us.

"'Do you know why humans fear spiders?' he'd said, and for all that I'd seen through my own ring, I found myself afraid. 'It is in part because they can move in any direction without warning. But in larger part because, for all their quickness, they choose to wait for their prey. A patient spider can defeat even the most powerful lion.'

"His orb weavers climbed the walls of our tent, and they began furiously spinning a web to enclose us. Esmerelda and I were terrified, but we dared not move. Mr. Eberly was clearly more powerful than we were.

"'In this book,' he'd said, removing from his coat the tome you discovered tonight, 'you will find the terrible history of the eight rings of the Order. Wealth, power, greed, and deceit are etched onto these pages. The powers of Anansi have led countless unsuspecting victims astray. But there is no one more greedy or deceitful than the present possessor of the Black Widow ring.'

"It seemed the Black Widow had been seeking out the other ring bearers and obtaining their rings at any cost. As Mr. Eberly put it, if he had found us so easily, the cunning Black Widow couldn't be far behind.

"I'm ashamed to admit it now, but Esmerelda and I thought Mr. Eberly was insane. It was not that his story made no sense, mind you — at that point, we'd begun to wonder ourselves whether these magical rings were entirely *decent*. It was more that his manner was so frantic, so absurd. He was a bad performer. We didn't know yet that the rings had that effect on everyone in the end. We were young, and this man was old."

This last line had been aimed squarely at Maria, surely. And true, she'd been thinking more and more that Arturo sounded crazy — paranoid like Grandma Esme always had been — even when his story explained so many things. But then, she herself had become a bit less sane since she first put on the Brown Recluse ring. Her behavior at Claire's party seemed proof of that.

"We didn't listen to his warnings, Maria. We thanked him, and said we would be more careful about whom we showed our rings. But we refused to cancel our performance that evening. He left us the book, hoping it would change our minds, and begged to see us again before our show. But that afternoon, we learned that Mr. Eberly had fallen from the tower of the castle of Tourbillon. Even then, we accepted the story that he was a madman who had suffered a terrible accident. We couldn't see it for the portent it was."

"Hang on," Maria said, jumping to her feet. "Where did you say this performance was?"

"In Sion. It's a mountain town in the corner of Switzerland, near Italy."

"And the Black Widow was there?"

Arturo nodded.

"She'd been following us for days — the Orb Weaver was just a bonus. That night, she was at our performance, waiting in the audience to spring her trap. Esmerelda's lion, Cocoa, saved our lives. Unfortunately, we couldn't save his."

"Wait. You mean the Black Widow . . ."

"I'm afraid so, Maria. The Black Widow had us surrounded. We wouldn't have stood a chance had it not been for Cocoa's sacrifice. He knew right away who was commanding the spiders. He leaped at her from the ring, and managed to take a piece of her with him."

As Arturo said this, he touched his right ear, and Maria gasped. The feeling had been building inside her ever since the funeral, when Luellen had held her hands as if she was searching them. A jewelry appraiser who wore a hat like a mask — Maria must have been grieving indeed not to have noticed it before.

"I think I know who the Black Widow is," she said. "I think I've met her."

Arturo grimaced, but he didn't look surprised. So he knew the Black Widow's real identity, too.

"It's Derek's aunt Luellen, isn't it? She told me at the funeral she'd seen you and Grandma Esme perform in Switzerland. I almost didn't believe her."

"Luellen chased us relentlessly in the years after that horrible night. Our lives became a nightmare game of cat and mouse, moving from one abandoned building and false identity to the next, never feeling like we could trust anyone we met."

"Why didn't you just leave the rings somewhere?" Maria asked. "Put a big sign on them that said, 'Here you go, now leave us alone'?"

"The thought did occur to us. But we knew too much. And the legacy of the rings is one of fear and distrust. The reason the Black Widow always kills her victims is that she doesn't want anyone left to oppose her. She only has power while she has the rings. She can't risk having an army rise up against her to take that power away."

That Maria had been in the same room with this woman, while her grandmother's casket had been resting less than ten feet away, made her want to scream.

"So what happened?" she asked Arturo, trying to piece together a complete picture of her grandmother. "I mean, one minute you and Grandma Esme are on the run together, the next minute, she's going to yoga on Tuesdays and Thursdays and organizing church functions on Wednesdays and Sundays."

Maria couldn't keep all the bitterness out of her voice. Maybe the anger rising in her chest was keeping her mounting fear at bay, or maybe it was just building alongside it. Either way, there was the fear, and there was the anger. Why had Grandma Esme left the ring for her? Why had she let Maria get trapped in her story, instead of taking it with her?

Arturo looked stricken. "You think I abandoned her, is that it? You think I left her here for Luellen to find? *I'm* the only reason she had a life here for as long as she did. *I'm* the only reason that —"

He broke off with a gutteral sound between a snarl and a sob. This was clearly a case he had made before, if only to himself. It wasn't as convincing as he wanted it to be.

Arturo took a deep breath and tugged at the sleeves of his suit coat. He really did look like an old little boy, if that made any sense. It was like after so many years in hiding, he had stopped growing up. He was Peter Pan's lost shadow.

"I knew the only way the Black Widow would leave Esmerelda alone was if she thought she was dead. And I knew the only way Esmerelda would let me go was if she thought *I* was dead. So I gave her a passport and an address in a small American city I hoped would remind her of Cahul, and I told her I'd meet her after a short detour."

"And that was the last time you saw her?"

"No," Arturo said. "But until last week, that was the last time she saw me."

CHAPTER 14

It was strange how so many things could finally make sense at the exact same moment that suddenly nothing made sense. It was like Maria had spent hours putting a puzzle together based on the picture on the box, only to get to the end and realize that the box didn't match the puzzle at all.

She continued to question Arturo. "Mom always said that Grandpa Lopez passed away before Dad was even born. I'm starting to think there was no Grandpa Lopez. Is that right?"

"You're a smart girl, Maria. Just like your grandmother."

"She knew Luellen was after her. She told me a week ago, 'The other spiders are back.' I thought she meant real spiders, the kind she collected. I had no idea she meant other people with rings."

"I came to her as soon as I knew Luellen was on her trail. I tried to get her to leave with me, to run. But she wouldn't."

"You tried to get Grandma Esme to leave us?" Maria asked, horrified.

"If she had come with me, she'd still be alive."

"Maybe, but that doesn't sound like much of a life to me. You can't just keep leaving your family behind whenever things get scary. That's not how it works."

As soon as she said it, she felt a stab of guilt. It was one thing to say this, and another to believe it. Her shoes were still caked with mud from her own late-night escape.

"Oh my gosh," she said, connecting the last of the puzzle pieces. "Luellen knows about the rest of my family, too. She even met them at the funeral."

Maria thought of how cruel she'd been to Rafi

earlier, not to mention the way she'd yelled at her mom. They'd only been looking out for her, when here she was, putting both of their lives in danger.

"Why hasn't the Black Widow tried to kill me yet?" Maria asked.

"I'm sure she is hoping to catch us both at once. I've eluded her for over seventy years, and she's growing impatient. If we are lucky, her impatience will make her careless."

"What do you mean, 'if we're lucky'? What do you plan for us to do?"

"Run away, of course! Haven't you heard a word I've said? The Black Widow is here, and you are fortunate to be alive. Especially after your extravagant choice of mourning clothes and your little temper tantrum at the birthday party. Honestly, Maria, I'll grant you your grandmother didn't fully explain the nature of the rings, but the way you've been broadcasting your powers this week —"

"Has been no worse than what you and Grandma Esme did back in the day," Maria said, cutting him off. She stood to her full height and brushed off her dress.

She crossed her arms so that the Brown Recluse ring glittered against her skin. "Now, thank you for all your help, but I am not running away. My best friend says that if something makes you nervous, it just means that you're thinking about it too much. And he is one of many people whose lives are in danger if we don't stay and fight the Black Widow."

"You mean Derek? I hate to tell you this, Maria, but I fear Derek has already become one of his aunt's followers."

Maria couldn't help laughing. "A follower? Derek? If there's one thing about Derek I can absolutely guarantee, it's that he does his own thing."

"This isn't a joke," Arturo bellowed. "I don't mean followers in the grammar-school playground sense of the word. More powerful men than Derek have been drawn into the Black Widow's web. And with six rings now in her possession, the Black Widow will surely have powers even beyond my imagining."

"Well," Maria said, her voice staying strong even as her eyes misted over, "that's all the more reason why he needs my help."

"Don't be foolish, Maria. I won't let you throw your life away like your grandmother did."

"Grandma Esme didn't throw her life away!" Maria roared. "She made a wonderful life here, and she fought to protect it. You ran away, but she stayed with what was important to her. She warned me that I'd face the same decision. To do what is easy and run away, or do what is right and stay. You can make your choice however you want to, but my mind is made up."

"I won't allow it. I'm sorry, Maria, but this is for your own good."

Arturo moved like smoke, twisting his body in a fluid arc that shouldn't have been possible at his age. In a blink, he had taken off his suit coat and thrown it at her, as if it was a net he could catch her in. Maria darted away without thinking, fleeing the cave with Arturo's footsteps thundering behind her.

Her spiders were screaming, *Hurry, hurry,* but it was nearly impossible for her to run — the mirror spiders were everywhere, their round silver bodies glittering in the dull light of the cave.

Maria darted and dodged, narrowly avoiding them with every step. She knew it too well — a spider never forgets. She could hear Arturo locked in the same struggle behind her, cursing the brown recluse spiders that had come to her defense.

Maria could see the mirror spiders scrambling to build a web in the mouth of the cave. Even if she pushed through, there was no way she could avoid them on the slippery staircase.

Yelling a warning to the spiders to get out of the way, Maria threw her arms in an arc and leaped.

CHAPTER 15

In less than a second, the icy-dark water came up to meet her.

Maria surfaced for air as fast as she could. The pool of deep water at the bottom of the fall was no bigger than her mom's jeep. Five feet to the right and Maria would have landed headfirst on the sharp rocks at the bottom.

Maria kicked her legs until she reached the edge of the sinkhole. She'd always hated swimming, and swimming in a dress was even worse. The wet silk of the skirt clung to her legs as she climbed out of the water and pulled herself up the slippery rocks to even ground. As soon as she was on her feet, she ran. She didn't look back.

The image in her mind of a swooping black coat and a sea of pale light was enough to keep her running.

She reached the boardwalk, and then the short grass, and then the line of her backyard. She was almost home free. But one look through the sliding glass door and Maria could tell something was wrong.

The lights were all on, and the chairs around the kitchen table were overturned. The refrigerator door stood open. Maria crept up to her house as quickly as she dared. She didn't hear anything from inside the house, which supported her suspicion that whoever had done this was already gone.

Not that she had any doubt who had done this.

Maria slid the glass door open. She stepped over the oranges, trash, forks, and knives that had been scattered across the floor, trying not to imagine the struggle that must have taken place while she was in the cave.

"Mom? Rafi?" she called. She wasn't surprised when they didn't answer.

She had sworn she wouldn't get trapped in Arturo's story, but that's exactly what had happened. It didn't matter that he probably thought he was on her side —

he and the Black Widow, and now Maria, too, were all part of the same vicious web. A poisonous circle that ensnared innocent people, just like the one around her finger.

Maria dripped water all the way back to her room, only now thinking to take off her shoes. Surely her mother would forgive her the muddy footprints, under the circumstances. For now, Maria needed to change clothes, and she needed to save her family. If she thought too hard about all the steps that came in between those two things, she might faint. Unfortunately, not overthinking things had always been Derek's strong suit, not hers.

When Maria flicked on her light switch, she had to stifle a scream. The spiderweb that had begun blooming on her bedroom ceiling days ago now stretched all the way across the room. In the center of the web was a small white rectangle.

On closer inspection, Maria recognized it as a business card for Vic's Antiques. Derek had once used a stack of these cards to do a magic trick. He'd had Maria write her name on one of them, then he'd put the whole stack behind his back and acted like he was trying to feel for which one had pen markings on it. Finally, he'd brought his hands back around to reveal that the card with the writing was the only one left in his hands at all. The rest of the stack had simply disappeared.

The business card in the center of the spiderweb didn't have any writing on it, but the message was clear enough. The Black Widow had sprung her trap. Rafi and Mom were the bait.

Maria drew back her arm and slung her shoes at the web. The sound of the wet smack as the shoes hit the wall gave her courage.

She felt the ring on her hand grow warm. She heard the spiders before she saw them, and for one paralyzing second, she thought that Arturo had found her — that she'd never get the chance to rescue her family.

But of course she could hear only her own spiders, and her fear turned into a sense of overwhelming relief as a brown recluse swarm surrounded her feet. Her reinforcements had arrived.

The spiders did not stop by her side, however.

Maria's ring grew from warm to hot, until it was almost painful, as the brown recluse spiders scurried up the wall to the web. The voices in her head were so fast and frenzied, it was impossible to untangle them. What Maria saw clearly was a color: red.

Maria followed her spiders as they climbed, until finally she saw what she had missed before — a black widow spider near the top of the web. It dangled from a thread over the hole Maria's shoe had just created. It seemed to be injured, or stuck, or afraid.

The brown recluse clutter flew at the lone black widow. In a second, they would be upon it, blind with rage.

"Wait, stop!" Maria shouted. "That's not what I wanted!"

Her spiders stopped. They turned to face her, confused.

"If you kill that spider, we will only pay the price later. Now, I'm sorry, but at the moment, what I really need is to go save my family, and I need your help. Will you come with me? Please?"

Her spiders hesitated. It seemed to Maria that they didn't care about the price — they wanted to eliminate their enemy. Maria hoped she wasn't abusing their friendship by telling them no. But then, a real friend sometimes *was* the one who told you what you didn't want to hear but needed to.

Finally, her spiders backed down, and the red in the back of Maria's mind became a much quieter blue. The black widow pulled itself up to the top part of the web, and it, too, looked at Maria, as if it was considering what to do with her.

"You can go now," Maria said, none too warmly. "But if I find you doing anything to my mom or brother, I'm not going to stop them next time."

The black widow fled, and the brown recluse spiders waited at attention.

"I'll meet you by the front door," Maria said, and as they left her alone, she took a deep breath. She was happy to have them with her, she thought. Now that she'd seen what they were capable of, she knew it was better than having them against her.

Maria changed into a pair of jeans and a T-shirt. It was after three in the morning, and she had reached that point in being tired where she was actually dizzy, as if she might fall asleep standing up. But no good could come of waiting. And the exhaustion was making her braver than she would be in the daylight.

She threw on a hoodie — one with a sewn-on sword patch that always reminded her of *Agatha at Sea* — and in this armor, headed out into the night.

CHAPTER 16

The historic district was deserted. Maria had been here at night plenty of times before, with Derek's family or for town festivals, but usually there were cars parked on the street, and other people around. Now the old streetlamps cast pale oranges and yellows on all the empty shops and restaurants, and the wide-open road looked like a set for a movie about the zombie apocalypse.

Maria stepped out of the shadows and hurried across the street before she could think better of it. Even the spiders trailing at her feet were nervous. Their energy crackled like a radio in her brain.

She reached the door to the shop at a jog, but the creepy doll in the display window stopped her cold. Its wooden horse mount was rocking back and forth as if it had only just been pushed. Maria could swear the doll was looking back at her.

Over the doll's shoulder, a picture caught Maria's eye. It was one of many old photographs on a corkboard in the display window. All of them had something to do with the history of the shop, and Maria had never paid them much attention before. But one of the photos was a family portrait from when Derek's great-grandpa Vic was a little boy. And now Maria noticed a girl next to Vic — a girl who looked so much like Aunt Luellen that they could be twins.

But they weren't twins, were they? This must be Luellen herself, already a teenager almost a hundred years ago. Maria had guessed that the rings had something to do with Arturo's and Grandma Esme's remarkable youth. But if this picture proved what Maria thought it did, the combined power of the rings had kept Luellen from aging hardly at all in a century. Perhaps with all eight rings, she'd become immortal.

Maria tried the door. As she expected, it wasn't locked. She pushed it open quickly. The sudden, frantic warnings of her spiders came a moment too late.

She ran headlong into a heavy black coat, which enveloped her even faster than she could scream.

Maria was thrown back outside, and she heard the door slam closed behind her. When the coat was yanked off, she was face-to-face with Arturo, who in this strange light looked like an alien, and not the friendly kind, either.

"What in the world is wrong with you?" he said, clenching his coat in his fist. "Did you really think you could just barge your way in there and take down the Black Widow by yourself?"

"I'm not by myself," Maria said defiantly. Her spiders twittered.

Arturo ran his hands through his hair and breathed an exasperated sigh.

"You're every bit as stubborn as your grandmother. I hope you know that. But even she would have approached this problem with a bit more forethought. You can't help your family at all by rushing in and getting yourself killed."

"Oh, so you're trying to help me now?"

"In my own way, yes."

He gave off the faintest hint of a smile, not devious or deceitful but perhaps a bit playful, as if to acknowledge just how peculiar *his way* was. In that smile, Maria could see the young man Grandma Esme had known.

He loved her, Maria thought. *He really did.*

"All right, then," she said. "So what now? I didn't see anyone else in the shop, and this was my only lead."

"Oh, someone's in the shop, all right. The light was on in the basement. My mirrors should be here any" — he cracked open the shop door, and a trio of shiny mirror spiders slinked out — "moment."

The spiders crawled up Arturo's leg, all the way to his shoulder. He squinted his eyes as if listening to a faraway sound.

"They say the boy is down there. Derek, it sounds like. But your mother and brother, too. The two of them are . . . *asleep.* My mirrors caught no sign of Luellen herself. I expect she is still out looking for you."

"Then what are we waiting for? Derek won't be a problem. He won't. I know it."

"Maria, I don't think you understand how dangerous a person without a mind of his own can be."

"Sure I do," Maria said. "This girl in my school, Claire, has turned practically the whole seventh grade into followers."

"If you don't take this seriously, you're going to get us *both* killed."

"I'm sorry, but look: You might know more about spiders, but I know more about Derek. If you just let me talk to him, I —"

"No. I have a better plan."

Every moment they spent talking in the street was a moment they weren't rescuing Rafi and Mom.

"Fine. What's your plan?"

"Well, part one is that we hide your ring."

"What?"

"Your ring. If you take it right to her, you have nothing left to bargain with, and she'll kill you immediately. If you hide it, you have the power to negotiate."

Maria winced. She hadn't thought about that. But there was one small problem.

"I'm sorry, but I don't trust you all the way. The

Black Widow kidnapped my family, but you tried to kidnap me, too, you know. Esme gave me the ring, so the ring stays with me."

Arturo narrowed his eyes at her, visibly unhappy.

"Fine," he seethed. "Then on to part two."

And with that, he turned and swept back into the shop, not even bothering to make sure Maria was following him. Fine by her. She was getting the hang of this Order thing. You just had to accept that everyone was trying to trick you at all times, and the only safe bet was to trick them back.

"Are you ready?" Maria whispered to her spiders. She could almost feel their anxious twitching in response. "Me neither," she said.

Arturo was waiting for her at the checkout counter inside. The light from the basement filtered up and speckled the main room with just enough slivers to see by. The same old trinkets that had looked so harmless and familiar earlier now looked like the possessions of ghosts.

"They say Derek is guarding your family on the far side of the room," Arturo whispered, the trio of spiders still perched on his shoulder. "I'll go down first and keep him occupied while you sneak around and free them. And whatever you see down in the basement, you mustn't stop moving. Do you think you can do that?"

"How are you going to distract him?"

"Do you think you can do that?" Arturo repeated.

Maria nodded. She dreaded to think what the mirror spiders had seen that Arturo was so afraid to tell her now.

"Then do it, and don't worry about how I'm going to distract him. Just count to ten, then follow me down the stairs."

With that, Arturo disappeared through the door.

One, two, three, Maria counted, listening for movement from the basement but hearing nothing.

"Stay close to me," she whispered to her spiders.

Four, five, six. Still nothing. Maria went to the door.

We will, her spiders whispered, and the ring grew warm.

Seven, eight, nine. She took a deep breath.

"Here goes nothing."

Ten.

She raced down the stairs to the sound of shattering glass.

CHAPTER 17

The scene in the basement took her totally by surprise.

It was all the same junk from before, but it had been reconfigured — organized, somehow, though into what Maria couldn't say. Across the room, Derek appeared to be strapped into a makeshift suit of armor comprised of pots, pans, and deconstructed furniture. The clock he'd been "repairing" earlier was now on his chest plate, counting time. He was wielding a fireplace poker like a sword, and the reckless anger in his movement as he struck out at Arturo was the only thing that kept the whole image from being comical.

Maria breathed in sharply as the poker connected with Arturo's chest, but the sound of her gasp was drowned out by more glass shattering. It hadn't been Arturo at all, but his reflection in one of the many old mirrors. By the looks of the shattered glass on the ground behind Derek, this had happened before.

She was still standing there, agog, when Derek started to turn his eyes in her direction. She'd been given one instruction — *don't get distracted* — and already she'd blown it. She was about to ruin the entire rescue.

Arturo appeared farther into the room, and he shouted, "Hey! Junk heap!" Derek whirred around in rage.

Maria ducked behind a nearby dresser, scrambling to take in the rest of her surroundings. She needed to find her mother and Rafi and get them out of here fast, before the Black Widow returned.

Then, in the corner, she saw something ghastly — something that robbed all the air from her lungs. It was the spiderweb to end all spiderwebs, strewn between the wooden beams that seemed to hold the whole foundation of the old building in place.

Mom and Rafi weren't just strung up in the web — they were wrapped from neck to foot, so that their faces were visible and visibly distressed. As the spiders had warned, neither of them appeared to be awake, which was probably a good thing. If Rafi were awake, he'd be hysterical. He never liked small spaces or being forced to keep still.

Maria made her way from one hiding spot to the next in a low crouch, dodging left and right as Derek turned with his weapon. Arturo was clearly trying to lead him away from the web, but he was limited by the placement and number of mirrors — a number that was getting smaller as Derek demolished one after another.

Finally, Maria reached the web. Up close, she could see that Rafi's lips were tinged with blue, and the color had drained from Mom's face. They couldn't be gone. They *couldn't*. Whatever was keeping them unconscious must have sent them into a kind of shock.

"A*ha*!" Derek shouted, parrying once more with the poker. The glass of one more mirror crashed with the resounding cascade of a chime, and a cuckoo clock somewhere in the rubble echoed in the silence that followed. But that was the last mirror, and when Derek spun on his heel, he was standing face-to-face with the real Arturo. Over Arturo's shoulder, Derek saw Maria, and he knew he'd been had.

"Maria, hurry!" Arturo called. She'd failed his orders *again*. She was just so tired, disoriented, and scared.

But she pushed on because she had to. She clawed at the web until it was thick in her fingernails. When her hands started to get stuck, she used her teeth.

"Help me," she pleaded, and her spiders went to work immediately. But this was no ordinary spiderweb; it was thick like plastic and almost as strong. If only she'd thought to bring a knife.

Meanwhile, Arturo struggled to keep Derek away using what looked like the leg of an old table. It was stranger than any duel Maria had ever imagined, and clumsier, louder, and more dangerous, too. Maria didn't want either of them to be hurt, but it was finally sinking in that this wasn't her best friend — the Black Widow's power had seen to that.

"Wake up, Rafi," Maria said desperately. "Help me get Mom down. *Please*, wake up."

But Rafi would not wake up. And even as Maria tugged and bit, and even as her own spiders struggled alongside her, she heard a scuttling sound, and she knew she was already too late. The enemy spiders were here, and they were out for blood.

In droves, they rushed over her hands and arms; they swarmed her face, knocking her glasses askew. Forced to let go of the web, Maria flailed about, trying to rid her body of the onslaught. But for every spider she shook off, two more appeared. Bulbous spiders, brown-and-red spiders — there were even bright yellow and glassy green spiders — all of them crawling on her skin with legs like little needles. And then there were black widow spiders, with their poison-red hourglasses.

In the moments when she could see her surroundings through the maelstrom of fear and color, she realized that the spiders were turning on Arturo as well. Arturo was stomping on the spiders left and right; he didn't seem to have any of Maria's qualms about hurting them. With each spider Arturo killed, the rest of the swarm became angrier and angrier.

When Maria finally felt the spiders moving in the same direction, and the direction was down and away from her body, she entertained the hope that they had changed their minds once more and decided to help her. But if that were the case, her own brown recluse spiders wouldn't sound so panicked. And what's more, she couldn't move her arms or legs. The enemy spiders had wrapped her in a web so tight, she could hardly breathe. Arturo looked to have suffered the same fate, and he was beyond miserable. After decades of successfully evading capture, he'd finally been caught, thanks to Maria's stupidity.

Derek was winded. He clutched his sides and gulped down air, and for a fraction of a second, he looked like the boy Maria knew. But then he stood upright and glowered at her, as if she had done something to him and not the other way around.

"Derek, help us out," Maria pleaded. "You don't have to do this, you know. This isn't who you are. We can get away from her."

"No. We can't." His voice was monotonous, impossible to interpret. "There's no escaping her. The Black Widow is everywhere, in us and around us."

And, as if fulfilling a prophecy or obeying a command, the spiders began to pool at Derek's feet, pouring out of the walls and the ceiling and the heaps of antiques. They scrambled to climb on top of one another, a mountain of spiders that grew higher and higher.

The teeming pile became tighter and denser, until it looked almost solid, and Maria couldn't distinguish one spider from the next. Then the pile began to take shape, squeezing in at the bottom and expanding out at the top, the very peak separating into long, thin bands like hair.

Finally, it wasn't a pile at all. It was a woman. It was Luellen.

Only it wasn't Luellen — there were a few key differences.

This woman had eight eyes and two terrible mandibles. The mandibles clacked together in a grotesque imitation of speech, and whether it was because words actually came out or because Maria was wearing her ring, she knew this was the Black Widow, and the Black Widow was hungry.

The Black Widow surveyed the room with those eight horrible eyes. She took her time, too, gloating in her victory.

"I have waited many years for this moment," she said. "But I knew the rings would come to me in the end." She turned to Arturo. "I think I will take the Brown Recluse first, so that I can savor killing you afterward. I have spent too much of my life hunting you down, oh amazing one, but it will hardly matter when I have all eight rings."

"You don't need to kill the girl," Arturo said. "Look at her — she's hardly a threat to you."

"She's as cunning and ruthless as I am, as we both well know. Besides, I don't do anything without doing it thoroughly."

The Luellen-like creature sauntered right up to Maria, its legs quivering with each step so that Maria could almost see the hundreds of spiders in its veins. Maria's terrified face was reflected back at her eight times.

"Don't worry, little one. This will only hurt for a second."

She raised her arm across her chest as if she was going to backhand Maria. Maria saw the lights glittering off all six rings, one on each finger except her middle finger, which had two. Luellen's fingers were long and sharp, like tiny daggers. There was no telling which of the rings produced that effect.

In the split second before the blow landed, Arturo disappeared with a *pop* and reappeared right before Maria. Luellen's hand came down with a sickly slice. Just like that, Arturo was dead.

"No!" Maria shouted, her voice breaking like a wave. Her anguish seemed finally to pierce Derek's armor. His eyes opened wide and he noticed the iron poker in his hand as if for the first time.

Luellen prodded Arturo's body with her foot, then leaned over to remove the Mirror Ring as if she were picking out a diamond from a pile of trash. She slid the ring onto her middle finger so that it now bore three. As soon as it did, Luellen's eyes glazed over with veils of red. Her transformation was nearly complete.

Luellen stared at her hand, then blinked all eight of her horrible red eyes at once. She turned her attention back to Maria.

"Symmetry, my dear, is everything in life. Balance, order, what-goes-around and all that jazz. There's nothing quite like a perfect circle, except perhaps a perfect story, which exists always in a loop, the infinite present. When you are gone, *I* will be the story. When you are gone, the Order of Anansi will begin and end with me. I am sure you can see the beauty in that."

Maria's spiders screamed their protest in her mind. They didn't think the Black Widow's vision for the future was beautiful. They were as frightened and appalled as Maria was.

"The Order won't end with you," Maria said. "You don't really control the spiders. They make the circle. You're just a cog."

For a moment, the Black Widow looked furious, her red eyes flashing dangerously. Then she threw back her head and laughed.

She removed the mirror ring, and her eyes became black once more. She removed another ring, and another, and her mandibles became cheeks and her eight eyes melded into two. At last, it was Luellen standing before her, not the Black Widow. She held the seven rings in her hand. In place of her right ear was a nub of flesh. And at her feet, an army of spiders stood ready to strike.

"Who is that pathetic little act for, Maria? Me? The spiders? My drudge of a nephew?"

Behind her and unnoticed, Derek blanched. Whatever spell the Black Widow had held over him was gone. A plan was quickly forming in Maria's mind. She just needed to keep Luellen talking.

"It isn't an act," Maria said. "It's the truth. My grandmother taught me never to harm a spider. How many have you killed to get those rings? How many more lives will you take when you have mine, too?"

"No more than you would have taken if I'd given you the chance. Oh, yes, Maria. My spies told me all about what happened at that little girl's birthday party. You wanted to make her suffer, and you did. You wanted to have an expensive dress like hers, so you commanded your spiders to make you one. You expect me to believe you're an innocent victim, but you're not, Maria. You're a wicked girl."

"I didn't mean to do that!" Maria shouted. "Or at least, I was sorry after I did it. That's the important thing." She hoped that was true. She had to believe it was.

"Oh, I'm sure the Brown Recluses before you were all *very sorry* when they eliminated their enemies, too. Did your grandmother happen to mention that of all the eight rings, the Brown Recluse has had the most violent history by far? No? Of course not. But so it goes. The venom of the brown recluse spider is far deadlier than the black widow's. It is no coincidence that the ring you wear is the only poison ring in the collection. So you'll forgive me for not believing your warmhearted display. I've already seen every trick in the book."

At that exact moment, Derek swung the fire iron.

But Luellen heard it coming, and she turned and caught the iron as if it were made of paper.

"Idiot boy," she snarled, snatching the poker from his hands and pushing him to the ground, where he was instantly overtaken by spiders.

Maria screamed, but she had no time to rescue her friend now — Luellen was jamming the rings back onto her fingers, and if Maria didn't think of something fast, she and her family were history.

Ripping out of her bonds with a desperate burst of adrenaline, she ran, only daring a look back after she rounded a corner of antiques.

The Black Widow whipped out her hand as if she were throwing a dart, and Maria flinched. But the Black Widow hadn't thrown anything at all; she had issued an order, and now her army was scrambling after Maria like desperate villagers fleeing a landslide. The glint of the mirror spiders newly under the Black Widow's command shone through the masses.

Maria could feel the vibrations of the approaching swarm, and she could feel the desperate buzzing of her brown recluse friends as they hurried to surround and defend her. Maria could see that it wouldn't be enough. She kept on running, crawling under a table and coming out in a crouch between two dressers. The floor was littered with shattered glass from where Arturo and Derek had battled not five minutes before. Her spiders surrounded her, awaiting her next instruction.

"Show yourself, girl. I grow tired of waiting."

Quietly, carefully, Maria crawled over to a tall wooden wardrobe. She was so close to the stairs leading up and outside. If she made a dash for it, she might be able to escape and come back when she had more help.

Run, her spiders said. *Run far and hide.*

"If you don't come out here right now, I'm going to start feeding your family and friend to my army. I think I'll start with your mother."

It was now or never. Fight or flee.

Flee, flee.

But she'd made her decision a long time ago. She'd promised her grandmother.

She got to her feet.

"You don't scare us," she called.

She stepped around the wardrobe. She could see the Black Widow in the center of the maze, waiting for Maria like the spider she was.

The swarm of enemy spiders scrambled up behind her. Her brown recluse spiders formed a circle at her feet, ready to defend, and her ring became hot with their wild energy.

The stage was set for a final performance.

"No, please," Maria said to her spiders. "You've done so much to help me and my family already. I don't want you risking your lives for me anymore. Thank you."

And with that, Maria took off her ring.

"Is this what you want?" she said to the Black Widow. "Well, you can have it!" She threw the ring as hard and as far as she could.

"No!" the Black Widow screamed, darting after it.

Maria seized her chance, running to the corner where her family — and now Derek — were strung up in the web. Derek was still awake and aware, at least. His eyes darted frantically in every direction.

"I'm here, don't worry," Maria said, even though she knew there was no way she was getting them down. The web was too tough. But they were together now, and that was all she wanted.

She heard the triumphant cry of the Black Widow behind her, and she knew it would be over soon — that she'd found the last ring.

Maria hugged her brother, her mom, and Derek, as best she could.

"I love you," she said. "I hope you know that."

She turned. The Black Widow stood facing her, not fifteen feet away. Her transformation was complete, and the sight was so horrible, Maria could barely look. Spiders — now including Maria's brown recluse friends — swarmed over and around her body, skittering at her feet.

"Now, my soldiers," the Black Widow said, "it is time to *feed*."

She pointed her terrible arms, and the spiders came at Maria in a streak like chain lightning. Maria closed her eyes, prepared for the end.

But then a second passed, and another.

Not only was she still alive, the room had gone silent.

Maria opened her eyes. The approaching army had stopped cold a mere two steps in front of her. Between the front ranks and Maria stood a single black widow spider.

Could it be —

Was it the spider from before?

"What are you doing?" the Black Widow snarled. "Feed, you fools! I gave you an order."

But the spiders did not move. With a surge of hope, Maria wondered if the black widow at her feet might be the very same spider whose life she'd spared in Grandma Esme's house. The same spider she'd let live in this very basement — the spider she'd saved in her house tonight.

Whatever this black widow was telling the others, it seemed to be working.

The brown recluse spiders broke away from the group, joining the black widow at Maria's side.

"She's just a little girl! Don't tell me you're afraid of her."

Without her ring, Maria couldn't know for sure, but she didn't think this was fear. This looked more like an act of friendship.

"Fine, I'll do it myself," the Black Widow said acidly. She took a step forward, stomping on a cluster of spiders without even a flicker of remorse. She took another step — *bam*. And another. And another.

Maria gasped. The spiders were angry. She didn't need a ring to see that.

The Black Widow went to take another step — the step that would bring her within striking distance of Maria — but the legion of spiders saw to it that her foot never hit the ground.

Like a cloud of locusts, they were upon her.

The last thing Maria saw, before she covered her ears and closed her eyes, was a poison-red hourglass on the Black Widow's inhuman face.

Her time was up.

"Maria?"

It was Derek's voice, cracked and scared. Maria opened her eyes. Only a fraction of the spiders from before remained. There was no trace of the Black Widow. The eight spider rings were in a cluster on the floor.

Maria turned to her friend and pulled at the webbing around his face. Derek had a gash in his forehead that didn't look too deep, and a bite mark on his neck that was large and red. He was, to put it mildly, a little shaken up.

"Maria, I thought — And then when those spiders

were coming at you, I was all — But then they went after my — after the —"

Derek couldn't say anything else. He was too overwhelmed.

"It's okay, Derek. It's all over now. I'm going to get you down from there."

One more time, Maria clawed at the web. But this time, the spiders — *all* the spiders — came to help her.

It was slightly terrifying. "Thank you," she said delicately. She had a feeling they could understand her, even without her ring.

One by one, Maria and the spiders brought down Derek, Rafi, and her mother. Their heartbeats were normal. Their breathing was normal. Still, Maria knew she needed to get them an ambulance right away.

"Derek, can I use your cell phone?"

"What? Oh, yeah." Derek fished out his phone and handed it to her. He was clearly still in a daze, and hadn't entirely stopped crying.

Maria told 9-1-1 where to find them, and repeatedly exclaimed that she couldn't fully explain what had happened. Then she handed the phone back to Derek.

Surely, her mom would let her have one of her own after this.

"Maria, I still don't understand what happened tonight. One minute, I was sitting in my room after Claire's birthday party, and the next, I'm down here with a fire iron and there are spiders everywhere."

"I'll give you the full version later. For now, let's just say your aunt was in a secret club with some really messed-up people."

"Maria, I'm so sorry. I had no idea. And I can't believe I yelled at you —"

"Derek, it's okay. Really. I'm glad you were there to keep me from doing something even more wicked."

Derek wrapped her in a hug.

"You're the least wicked person I know," he said.

Maria smiled. This was exactly the right response.

Derek cleared his throat in Maria's ear, and Maria realized that the brown recluse spiders — along with the others — were standing there watching them. Perhaps they were waiting for their next command. Derek eyed them nervously.

"Do you . . . do you know what they want?"

"Nope," Maria said. She nodded at the rings. "I would need those to know that."

"You don't think . . . I mean, they're not going to . . . *eat us* . . . are they?"

"I don't think so," Maria said. "I don't think they liked how Luellen had been treating them. You can use a ring to make an obedient animal, but only a friend will help you in the end."

"Oh, yeah? So you'll be there for me next time I get mixed up in an unspeakable evil?"

"Always," Maria said. "I hope you know that."

CHAPTER 18

There was something wonderful about being on a boat.

The fishing pond in Falling Waters was no private lake, but the important thing today was that the Lopez family was here together, on their very own boat. Well, the Lopez family plus its honorary fourth member, Derek.

Their little boat rocked as Rafi's line went taut on a catch. The sun beat down on them, focusing extra hard on Maria's black jeans and T-shirt. She hardly minded. For one thing, she could see in a full circle around them, and what she didn't see was a single shadow or spider.

"What'd you catch?" Mom asked as Rafi reeled in his line.

"Looks like a catfish," Derek said.

"A tiny one," Rafi said. "I'm going to let it go." He unhooked the fish and threw it back in the water. He had done this five other times already, claiming that each fish was either too small to eat, too big to carry, or else too sad-looking.

Rafi had been acting different in the week since last Saturday. For one thing, he'd been noticeably nicer to Maria, which was all well and good. But he was also a little quieter, and a little jumpier, too. Maria hoped these changes would undo themselves in time. But it had been nice to hear him on the phone today, telling Rob that he didn't have time to hang out because he was going fishing with his own family.

"You know, you haven't touched your book since we got out here," Mom said to Maria.

"I didn't want to be rude. Besides, I only brought it out here because I thought fishing was supposed to be a silent activity. But you three have been talking nonstop since we stepped in the boat."

This was Maria's poor attempt at a joke. In truth, Mom had been a little quieter, too. Mercifully, neither she nor Rafi remembered *everything* about that night. But they remembered enough to know that Maria had saved them from something they weren't entirely sure they believed in.

"There's just something about still water that makes you feel like you have to whisper," Derek said. "It's like being in church."

"That reminds me," Mom said, "I've been thinking about how much I liked the people at Grandma Esme's church. They were just so welcoming. What would you guys say if we started going to that one on Sundays? Maybe pick up the Meals on Wheels program?"

"Sure," Rafi said.

"Sounds good to me," Maria agreed. Mom had been suggesting all kinds of little changes in the past few days, from family game night to Taco Tuesdays. They'd bought this boat before they even had the money from Grandma Esme's house, which they were definitely selling. Maria was fine with this, having finally decided that it was probably healthy to keep memories of a person in your heart, instead of in their objects. Then again, she was still wearing the purple pendant necklace today, and she'd placed the old anchor whistle on the same cord, deciding it was the exact kind of jewelry one should wear in a boat.

"So, um, Maria?" Rafi said. "The man . . . Arturo? He was our grandfather, but he wasn't a Lopez?"

Maria nodded.

"His real last name was Antonescu. He told me so in a story. But I think Grandma Esme would have wanted us to stay Lopezes. Don't you, Mom?"

"I do," Mom said. "And I, for one, like that our name starts with our little family."

The police investigation had finally ended this week when the wound on Arturo's neck had tested positive for black widow venom. It was determined that Rafi and Mom had been saved by the age difference and Maria's 9-1-1 call. Whatever the officials wanted to believe was fine by Maria. She had no interest in reliving the real details for anyone. Rafi and Mom hadn't even asked how they'd come to be in the basement of Vic's Antiques, which officially had been renamed Derek's Junk Shop two days ago. They were celebrating the living.

"Rob's parents said it was lucky the spiders at Claire's party weren't the same kind that bit us. She just had the regular scared-of-spiders kind of fainting."

"Oh, Claire," Derek said. "How long do you think it will be before she starts being mean again?"

"I think it might be a while this time," Maria said. "I told her I was sorry for telling people she had followers instead of friends, and she said she was sorry for the locker thing."

Derek flinched at the word *followers*, but Maria shrugged.

Maria reached into her pocket and pulled out a handful of rings. The sight of them made everyone nervous. Rafi clearly thought they were real spiders at first.

"What are you doing with those, Maria?" Mom said.

"I think I'm getting rid of them," she said.

"That's probably for the best." As soon as Mom had woken up in the hospital, she'd said to Maria, "Your grandmother warned us," then immediately fallen asleep again.

"Are you sure?" Derek said. "Those rings could make you rich forever. I mean, after you sell them, of course," he hastened to add. Mom and Rafi still had no idea that the rings had powers.

Maria shrugged. Money wasn't everything. It certainly wasn't worth the life that these accursed rings bought.

"Can I see them one last time?" Derek said.

Maria hesitated. She'd kept the rings hidden from everyone this week, locked in a trunk where not even the spiders could get them. They were just too tempting.

"Okay," she said, handing him the rings. "But just for a second."

Derek took them and looked at them. Each ring was a little different, in its own horrible way. Maria hadn't spent much time examining them.

Then Derek put them behind his back and moved his hands around.

"Guess which hand the Brown Recluse is in," he said.

"That's not funny, Derek." Maria reached out her palm for him to give them all back.

Her voice must have sounded awfully frantic, because right away Derek stopped and gave her back the rings. "I was just teasing you," he said.

Maria took the rings in her hands, and brought her hands to her mouth. There were no spiders in sight, but she hoped, after everything, that they would be able to hear her.

Thank you, she thought. *Thank you for everything. I don't have much to give you, but I can give you this.*

Without looking closely, Maria hurled the rings into the water.

Her mother gasped, and her brother gave her an odd look, but Maria didn't care. She had all the gifts she needed right here, in this little boat.

THE EIGHT RINGS OF ANANSI

The Orb Weaver

The Lynx Spider

The Crab Spider

The Wolf Spider

The Cobweb Spider

The Mirror Spider

The Brown Recluse

The Black Widow

ACKNOWLEDGMENTS

Thank you to . . .

My editor, David — you gave me light.

My team at Scholastic, and especially Jana Haussmann — you made this all possible.

My friends Joe, Jess, Zach, Nathan, Adam, Dan, and Nick — the story came to life first in your voices.

My friend Annie Swank — you always set the metrics.

My wonderful family — you are my magic ring.